HORRiD HENRY

ON THE GO

Meet HORRID HENRY
the laugh-out-loud
worldwide sensation!

....

★ Over 15 million copies sold in 27 countries and counting

★ # 1 chapter book series in the UK

★ Francesca Simon is the only American author to ever win the Galaxy British Book Awards Children's Book of the year (past winners include J. K. Rowling, Philip Pullman, and Eoin Colfer).

"A loveable bad boy."
—People

"Horrid Henry is a fabulous antihero...**a modern comic classic**." —*Guardian*

"**Wonderfully appealing to girls and boys alike**, a precious rarity at this age." —Judith Woods, *Times*

"The best children's comic writer."
—Amanda Craig, *Times*

"**I love the Horrid Henry books by Francesca Simon.** They have lots of funny bits in. And Henry always gets into trouble!" —Mia, age 6

"My two boys love this book, and **I have actually had tears running down my face and had to stop reading because of laughing so hard**." —T. Franklin, parent

"**Fine fare for beginning readers**, this clever book should find a ready audience." —*Booklist*

"**The angle here is spot-on, and reluctant readers will especially find lots to love about this early chapter book series**. Treat young readers to a book talk or read-aloud and watch Henry go flying off the shelf." —*Bulletin of the Center for Children's Books*

"I have tried out the Horrid Henry books with groups of children as a parent, as a baby-sitter, and as a teacher. **Children love to either hear them read aloud or to read them themselves**." —Danielle Hall, teacher

"A flicker of recognition must pass through most teachers and parents when they read Horrid Henry. **There's a tiny bit of him in all of us**." —Nancy Astee, *Child Education*

"**As a teacher...it's great to get a series of books my class loves**. They go mad for Horrid Henry." —teacher

"**Short, easy-to-read chapters will appeal to early readers, who will laugh at Henry's exaggerated antics and relate to his rambunctious personality**." —*School Library Journal*

"An absolutely fantastic series and surely a winner with all children. Long live Francesca Simon and her brilliant books! More, more please!"

—parent

"**Laugh-out-loud reading for both adults and children alike**." —parent

"**Henry's over-the-top behavior, the characters' snappy dialogue and Ross's hyperbolic line art will engage even the most reluctant readers—there's little reason to suspect the series won't conquer these shores as well**." —*Publishers Weekly*

Horrid Henry by Francesca Simon

HORRID HENRY
ON THE GO

Francesca Simon
Illustrated by Tony Ross

"Horrid Henry and the Zombie Vampire" originally appeared in *Horrid Henry and the Zombie Vampire*, text © Francesca Simon 2011, illustrations © Tony Ross 2011

"Horrid Henry Rocks" and "Moody Margaret's Sleepover" originally appeared in *Horrid Henry Rocks*, text © Francesca Simon 2010, illustrations © Tony Ross 2010

"Horrid Henry's Horrid Weekend" originally appeared in *Horrid Henry's Monster Movie*, text © Francesca Simon 2012, illustrations © Tony Ross 2012

"Horrid Henry Wakes the Dead" originally appeared in *Horrid Henry Wakes the Dead*, text © Francesca Simon 2009, illustrations © Tony Ross 2009

"Horrid Henry's Car Journey" originally appeared in *Horrid Henry and the Scary Sitter*, text © Francesca Simon 2002, illustrations © Tony Ross 2002

"Horrid Henry and the Abominable Snowman" originally appeared in *Horrid Henry and the Abominable Snowman*, text © Francesca Simon 2007, illustrations © Tony Ross 2007

"Horrid Henry Goes Shopping" originally appeared in *Horrid Henry and the Soccer Fiend*, text © Francesca Simon 2006, illustrations © Tony Ross 2006

"Horrid Henry Dines at Restaurant Le Posh" and "Horrid Henry's Hike" originally appeared in *Horrid Henry and the Mega-Mean Time Machine*, text © Francesca Simon 2005, illustrations © Tony Ross 2005

Cover and internal design © 2013 by Sourcebooks, Inc.

Published by Sourcebooks Jabberwocky, an imprint of Sourcebooks, Inc.
P.O. Box 4410, Naperville, Illinois 60567-4410
(630) 961-3900
Fax: (630) 961-2168
www.jabberwockykids.com

Library of Congress Cataloging-in-Publication data is on file with the publisher.

Source of Production: Versa Press, East Peoria, Illinois, USA
Date of Production: December 2012
Run Number: 19470

Printed and bound in the United States of America.
VP 10 9 8 7 6 5 4 3 2 1

CONTENTS

HORRID HENRY AND THE ZOMBIE VAMPIRE

....

"Isn't it exciting, Henry?" asked Perfect Peter, packing Bunnykins carefully in his Sammy the Snail overnight bag. "A museum sleepover! With a spooky flashlight walk! And work sheets! I can't think of anything more fun."

"I can," snarled Horrid Henry. Being trapped in a cave with Clever Clare reciting all the multiplication tables from one to a million. Watching *Cooking Cuties*. Even visiting Nurse Needle for one of her horrible injections. (Well, maybe not *that*.)

But *almost* anything would be better

than being stuck overnight in Our
Town Museum on a class sleepover. No
TV. No computers. No comics. Why
oh why did he have to do this? He
wanted to sleep in his own comfy bed,
not in a sleeping bag on the museum's
cold, hard floor, surrounded by photos
of old mayors and a few dusty exhibits.

AAARRRRGGGHH. Wasn't it bad
enough he was bored all day in school
without being bored all night too?

Worse, Peter's diaper baby class was
coming too. They'd probably have to
be tucked in at
seven o'clock,
when they'd all
start crying for
their mamas. Ugghh.
And then Miss Battle-
Axe snarling at them to
finish their work sheets,

Waaaaaaaa!

and Moody Margaret snoring, and
Anxious Andrew whimpering that he'd
seen a ghost…

Well, no way was he going to that
boring old dump without some comics
to pass the time. He'd just bought the
latest *Screamin' Demon* with a big article
all about vampires and zombies. Yay!
He couldn't wait to read it.

Perfect Peter watched him stuff his
Mutant Max bag full of comics.

"Henry, you know we're
not allowed to bring comics
to the museum sleepover,"
said Perfect Peter.

"Shut up and mind your
own business, toad," said
Horrid Henry.

"Mom! Henry just called
me a toad!" wailed Peter.
"And he told me to shut up."

"Toady toady toady, toady toady toady," jeered Henry.

"Henry! Stop being horrid or no museum sleepover for you," yelled Mom.

Horrid Henry paused. Was it too late to be horrid enough to get banned from the sleepover? Why hadn't he thought of this before? Why, he could...

"Henry! Peter! We have to leave *now!*" yelled Dad.

Rats.

The children lined up in the museum's central hall clutching their sleeping bags as Miss Lovely and Miss Battle-Axe ticked off names on a big register.

"Go away, Susan," said Moody Margaret. "After what you did at my house I'm going to sit with Gurinder. So there."

"You're such a meanie, Margaret," said Sour Susan.

4

"Am not."

"Are too."

Susan scowled. Margaret was *always* so mean. If only she could think of a way to pay that old grouch back.

Margaret scowled. Susan was *always* so annoying. If only she could think of a way to pay that old fraidy-cat back.

Henry scowled. Why did he have to be here? What he'd give for a magic carpet to whisk him straight home to the comfy black chair to watch *Terminator Gladiator*. Could life get any worse?

"Henwy," came a little voice next to him. "I love you Henwy. I want to give you a big kiss."

Oh no, thought Horrid Henry. Oh no. It was Lisping Lily, New Nick's little sister. What was that foul fiend doing here?

"You keep away from me," said

Horrid Henry, pushing and shoving his way through the children to escape her.

"Waaa!" wept Weepy William as Henry stepped on his foot.

"I want my mama," cried Needy Neil as Henry trampled on his sleeping bag.

"But I want to marry with you, Henwy," lisped Lily, trying to follow him.

"Henry! Stay still!" barked Miss Battle-Axe, glaring at him with her demon eyes.

"Hello, boys and girls, what an adventure we're going to have tonight," said the museum's guide, Earnest Ella, as she handed out pencils and work sheets.

Henry groaned. Boring! He hated work sheets.

"Did you know that our museum has a famous collection

7

of balls of wool through the ages?"
droned Earnest Ella. "And an old
railway car? Oh yes, it's going to be an
exciting sleepover night. We're even
going on a walk through the corridors
with only flashlights."

Horrid Henry yawned and sneaked
a peek at his comic book, which he'd
hidden beneath his museum work sheet.

**Watch out, demon fans!! To celebrate the
release of this season's big blockbuster monster
horror film, THE ZOMBIE VAMPIRES,
study this checklist. Make sure there are no
zombie vampires lurking in your neighborhood!!!!**

Horrid Henry gasped as he read
How to Recognize a Vampire and *How to
Recognize a Zombie*. Big, scary teeth?
Big, googly eyes? Looks like the
walking dead? Wow, that described

Miss Battle-Axe perfectly. All they had to add was a big fat carrot nose and…

A dark shadow loomed over him.

"I'll take that," snapped Miss Battle-Axe, yanking the comic out of his hand. "*And* the rest."

Huh?

He'd been so careful. How had she spotted that comic under his work

sheet? And how did she know about the secret stash in his bag? Horrid Henry looked around the hall. Aha!

There was Peter, pretending not to look at him. How dare that wormy worm toad tell on him? Just for that...

"Come along, everyone, line up to collect your flashlights for our spooky walk," said Earnest Ella. "You wouldn't want to get left behind in the dark, would you?"

There was no time to lose. Horrid Henry slipped over to Peter's class and joined him in line with Tidy Ted and Goody-Goody Gordon.

"Hello, Peter," said Henry sweetly.

Peter looked at him nervously. Did Henry suspect *he'd* told on him? Henry didn't *look* angry.

"Shame my comic got confiscated," said Henry, "'cause it had a list of how to tell whether anyone you know is a zombie vampire."

"A zombie vampire?" asked Tidy Ted.

10

"Yup," said Henry.

"They're imaginary," said Goody-Goody Gordon.

"That's what they'd *like* you to believe," said Henry. "But I've discovered some."

"Where?" said Ted.

Horrid Henry looked around dramatically, then dropped his voice to a whisper.

"Two teachers at our school," hissed Henry.

"Two *teachers?*" said Peter.

"What?" said Ted.

"You heard me. Zombie vampires. Miss Battle-Axe *and* Miss Lovely."

"Miss *Lovely*?" gasped Peter.

"You're just making that up," said Gordon.

"It was all in *Screamin' Demon*," said Henry. "That's why Miss Battle-Axe grabbed my comic. To stop me from finding out the truth. Listen carefully."

Henry recited:

"How to recognize a vampire:

1. BIG HUGE SCARY TEETH.

"If Miss Battle-Axe's fangs were any bigger she would trip over them," said Horrid Henry.

Tidy Ted nodded. "She *does* have big pointy teeth."

"That doesn't prove anything," said Peter.

"2. DRINKS BLOOD."

Perfect Peter shook his head. "Drinks... blood?"

"*Obviously* they do, just not *in front* of people," said Horrid Henry. "That would give away their terrible secret."

"3. ONLY APPEARS AT NIGHT."

"But Henry," said Goody-Goody Gordon, "we see Miss Battle-Axe and Miss Lovely every day at school. They *can't* be vampires."

Henry sighed. "Have you been paying attention? I didn't say they were *vampires*, I said they were *zombie* vampires. Being half-zombie lets them walk around in daylight."

Perfect Peter and Goody-Goody Gordon looked at one another.

"Here's the total proof," Henry continued.

"How to recognize a zombie:

1. LOOKS DEAD.

"Does Miss Battle-Axe look dead? Definitely," said Horrid Henry. "I never saw a more dead-looking person."

"But Henry," said Peter. "She's alive."

Unfortunately, yes, thought Horrid Henry.

"Duh," he said. "Zombies always *seem* alive. Plus, zombies have scary, bulging eyes like Miss Battle-Axe," continued Henry. "And they feed on human flesh."

"Miss Lovely doesn't eat human flesh," said Peter. "She's a vegetarian."

"A likely story," said Henry.

"You're just trying to scare us," said Peter.

"Don't you see?" said Henry. "They're planning to pounce on us during the flashlight walk."

"I don't believe you," said Peter.

Henry shrugged. "Fine. Don't believe me. Just don't say I didn't warn you when Miss Lovely lurches out of the dark and BITES you!" he shrieked.

"Be quiet, Henry," shouted Miss Battle-Axe. "William. Stop weeping. There's nothing to be scared of. Linda! Stand up. It's not bedtime yet. Bert! Where's your flashlight?"

"I dunno," said Beefy Bert.

Miss Lovely walked over and smiled at Peter.

"Looking forward to the flashlight walk?" she beamed.

Peter couldn't stop himself sneaking a peek at her teeth. *Were* they big? And sharp? Funny, he'd never noticed before how pointy two of them were… And was her face a bit…umm…pale?

No! Henry was just trying to trick him. Well, he wasn't going to be fooled.

"Time to go exploring," said Earnest Ella. "First stop on the shadowy trail: our brand-new exhibit, *Wonderful World of Wool*. Then we'll be popping next door down the *Passage to the Past* to visit the old railway car and the Victorian shop and a Neanderthal cave. Flashlights on, everyone."

Sour Susan smiled to herself. She'd
just thought of the perfect revenge on
Margaret for teasing her for being such
a scaredy-cat.

Moody Margaret smiled to herself.
She'd just thought of the perfect
revenge on Susan for being so sour.

Ha ha, Margaret, thought Susan.
I'll get you tonight.

Ha ha, Susan, thought Margaret.
I'll get you tonight.

Ha ha, Peter, thought Henry. I'll get
you tonight.

"Follow me," said Earnest Ella.

The children stampeded after her.

All except three.

When the coast was clear,
Moody Margaret turned off her
flashlight, darted into the pitch-
black *Passage to the Past* hall,
and hid in the Neanderthal cave
behind the caveman. She'd leap
out at Susan when she walked past.
MWAHAHAHAHAHAHA! Wouldn't
that old scaredy-cat get a fright.

Sour Susan turned off her flashlight
and peeked down the *Passage to the Past*
corridor. Empty. She tiptoed to the
railway car and crept inside. Just wait
till Margaret walked by…

Horrid Henry turned off his flashlight,
crept down the *Passage to the Past*,
sneaked into the Victorian shop, and
hid behind the rocking chair.

Tee-hee. Just wait till Peter walked past. He'd—

What was that?

Was it his imagination? Or did that spinning wheel in the corner of the shop...move?

CR—EEEK went the wheel.

It was so dark. But Henry didn't dare switch on his flashlight.

Moody Margaret looked over from the Neanderthal cave at the Victorian

shop. Was it her imagination or
was that rocking chair rocking back
and forth?

Sour Susan looked out
from the railway
car. Was it her
imagination or
was the caveman
moving?

There was a
strange, scuttling
noise.

What was that?
thought Susan.

You know, thought Henry, this
museum *is* kind of creepy at night.

And then something grabbed onto
his leg.

"AAAARRRRGGHHH!" screamed
Horrid Henry.

★ ★ ★

Moody Margaret heard a blood-curdling scream. Scarcely daring to breathe, Margaret peeped over the caveman's shoulder…

Sour Susan heard a blood-curdling scream. Scarcely daring to breathe, Susan peeped out from the railway carriage…

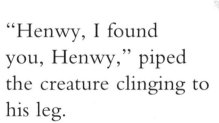

"Henwy, I found you, Henwy," piped the creature clinging to his leg.

"Go away, Lily," hissed Henry. The horrible fiend was going to ruin everything.

"Will you marry me, Henwy?"

"No!" said Horrid Henry, trying to

21

shake her off and brushing against the spinning wheel.

CR—EEEEK.

The spinning wheel spun.

What's that noise? thought Margaret, craning to see from behind the caveman.

"Henwy! I want to give you a big kiss," lisped Lily.

Horrid Henry shook his leg harder.

The spinning wheel tottered and fell over.

CRASH!

Margaret and Susan saw something lurch out of the Victorian shop and loom up in the darkness. A monstrous creature with four legs and waving arms…

"AAAARRRRGGHH!" screamed Susan.

"AAAARGGHHHHH!" shrieked Margaret.

"AAAARGGHHHHH!" shrieked Henry.

The unearthly screams rang through the museum. Peter, Ted, and Gordon froze.

"You don't think—" gasped Gordon.

"Not…" trembled Peter.

"Zombie vampires?" whimpered Ted. They clutched one another.

"Everyone head back to the Central Hall NOW!" shouted Earnest Ella.

In the cafeteria, Miss Lovely and Miss Battle-Axe were sneaking a short break to enjoy a lovely fried egg sandwich with lashings of ketchup.

Oh my weary bones, thought Miss Battle-Axe, as she sank her teeth into the huge sandwich. Peace at last.

AAARRGGHH! EEEEEKKK! HELLLP!

Miss Battle-Axe and Miss Lovely squeezed their sandwiches in shock as they heard the terrible screams.

SPLAT!

A stream of ketchup squirted Miss Lovely in the eye and dripped down her face onto her blouse.

SQUIRT!

A blob of ketchup splatted Miss Battle-Axe on the nose and dribbled down her chin onto her cardigan.

"Sorry, Boudicca," said Miss Lovely.

"Sorry, Lydia," said Miss Battle-Axe.

They raced into the dark central hall just as their classes ran back from the flashlight walk. Fifty beams of light from fifty flashlights lit up the teachers'

ketchup-covered faces and ketchup-stained clothes.

"AAAARRGGHHH!" screamed Perfect Peter.

"It's the zombie vampires!" howled Tidy Ted.

"Run for your lives!" yelped Goody-Goody Gordon.

"Wait!" shouted Miss Lovely. "Children, come back!"

"We won't eat you!" shouted Miss Battle-Axe.

"AAAARRRRGGHHHHHH!"

HORRID HENRY DINES AT RESTAURANT LE POSH

"Great news, everyone," said Mom, beaming. "Aunt Ruby is taking us all out for dinner to Le Posh, the best French restaurant in town."

"Oh boy, Restaurant Le Posh," said Perfect Peter. "We've never been there."

Horrid Henry stopped scribbling all over Peter's stamp album. His heart sank. French? Restaurant? Oh no. That meant strange, horrible, yucky food. That meant no burgers, no ketchup, no pizza. That meant—

"NOOOOOOOOOOO! I don't want

to go there!" howled Henry. Who knew what revolting poison would arrive on his plate, covered in gloopy sauce with green pieces floating around. Uggghh.

"It's Mom's birthday," said Dad, "so we're celebrating."

"I only like Whopper Whoopee," said Henry. "Or Fat Frank's. I don't want to go to Le Posh."

"But Henry," said Perfect Peter, tidying up his toys, "it's a chance to try new food."

Mom beamed. "Exactly, Peter. It's always nice to try new things."

"No it isn't," snarled Horrid Henry. "I hate trying new food when there's nothing wrong with the old."

"I love it," said Dad. "I eat everything except tomatoes."

"And I eat everything except squid," said Mom.

"And I love all vegetables except beets," said Perfect Peter. "Especially spinach and sprouts."

"Well I don't," shrieked Horrid Henry. "Do they have pasta?"

"Whatever they have will be delicious," said Mom firmly.

"Do they have burgers? If they don't I'm not going," wailed Horrid Henry.

Mom looked at Dad.

Dad looked at Mom.

Last time they'd taken Henry to a fancy restaurant he'd had a tantrum under the table. The time before he'd run screaming around the room

snatching all the salt and pepper shakers
and then threw up on the people at
the next table. The time before that—
Mom and Dad preferred not to think
about that.

"Should we get a babysitter?"
murmured Dad.

"Leave him home on my birthday?"
murmured Mom. She allowed herself
to be tempted for a moment. Then
she sighed.

"Henry, you are coming and you will
be on your best behavior," said Mom.
"Your cousin Steve will be there. You
wouldn't want Steve to see you make a
fuss, would you?"

 The hairs on the
back of Henry's
neck stood up.
Steve! Stuck-Up
Steve!

Horrid Henry's archenemy and the world's worst cousin. If there was a slimier boy than Steve slithering around then Horrid Henry would eat worms.

Last time they'd met Henry had tricked Steve into thinking there was a monster under his bed. Steve had sworn revenge. There was nothing Steve wouldn't do to get back at Henry.

Boy, did Horrid Henry hate Stuck-Up Steve.

Boy, did Stuck-Up Steve hate Horrid Henry.

"I'm not coming and that's final!" screamed Horrid Henry.

"Henry," said Dad. "I'll make a deal with you."

"What deal?" said Henry. It was always wise to be suspicious when parents offered deals.

"I want you to be pleasant and talk to

31

everyone. And you will eat everything on your plate like everyone else without making a fuss. If you do, I'll give you $2."

Two dollars! Two whole dollars! Horrid Henry gasped. Two whole dollars just for talking and shoving a few mouthfuls of disgusting food in his mouth. Normally he had to do that for free.

"How about $3?" said Henry.

"Henry..." said Mom.

"OK, deal," said Horrid Henry. But I won't eat a thing and they can't make me, he thought. He'd find a way. Dad said he had to eat everything on his plate. Well, maybe some food wouldn't *stay* on his plate...Horrid Henry smiled.

Perfect Peter stopped putting away his blocks. He frowned. Shouldn't *he* get two dollars like Henry?

"What's *my* reward for being good?" said Perfect Peter.

"Goodness is its own reward," said Dad.

The restaurant was hushed. The tables were covered in snowy-white

tablecloths, with yellow silk chairs. Huge gold chandeliers dangled from the ceiling. Crystal glasses twinkled. The rectangular china plates sparkled. Horrid Henry was impressed.

"Wow," said Henry. It was like walking into a palace.

"Haven't you ever been here before?" sneered Stuck-Up Steve.

"No," said Henry.

"*We* eat here all the time," said Steve. "I guess you're too poor."

"It's 'cause *we'd* rather eat at Whopper Whoopee," lied Henry.

"Hush, Steve," said Rich Aunt Ruby. "I'm sure Whopper Whoopee is a lovely restaurant."

Steve snorted.

Henry kicked him under the table.

"OWWWW!" yelped Steve. "Henry kicked me!"

"No I didn't," said Henry. "It was an accident."

"Henry," said Mom through gritted teeth. "Remember what we said about best behavior? We're in a fancy restaurant."

Horrid Henry scowled. He looked cautiously around. It was just as he'd feared. Everyone was busy eating weird pieces of this and that, covered in gloopy sauces. Henry checked under the tables to see if anyone was throwing up yet.

There was no one lying poisoned under the tables. I guess it's just a matter of time, thought Henry grimly. You won't catch me eating anything here.

Mom, Dad, Peter, and Rich Aunt Ruby blabbed away at their end of the table. Horrid Henry sat sullenly next to Stuck-Up Steve.

"I've got a new bike," Steve bragged. "Do you still have that old rust bucket you had last Christmas?"

"Hush, Steve," said Rich Aunt Ruby.

Horrid Henry's foot got ready to kick Steve.

"Boudicca Battle-Axe! How many times have I told you—don't chew with your mouth open," boomed a terrible voice.

Horrid Henry looked up. His jaw dropped.

There was his terrifying teacher, Miss

Battle-Axe, sitting at a small table in the corner with her back to him. She was with someone even taller, skinnier, and more ferocious than she was.

"And take your elbows off the table!"

"Yes, Mom," said Miss Battle-Axe meekly.

Henry could not believe his ears. Did teachers have mothers? Did teachers ever leave the school? Impossible.

"Boudicca! Stop slouching!"

"Yes, Mom," said Miss Battle-Axe, straightening up a fraction.

"So, what's everyone having?"

beamed Aunt Ruby. Horrid Henry tore
his eyes away from Miss Battle-Axe
and stared at the menu. It was entirely
written in French.

"I recommend the mussels," said Aunt
Ruby.

"Mussels! Ick!"
shrieked Henry.

"Or the blah blah
blah blah blah." Aunt
Ruby pronounced a few
mysterious French words.

"Maybe," said Mom. She looked a
little uncertain.

"Maybe," said Dad. He looked a little
uncertain.

"You order for me, Aunt Ruby," said Perfect Peter. "I eat everything."

Horrid Henry had no idea what food Aunt Ruby had suggested, but he knew he hated every single thing on the menu.

"I want a burger," said Henry.

"No burgers here," said Mom firmly. "This is Restaurant Le Posh."

"I said I want a burger!" shouted Henry. Several diners looked up.

"Don't be horrid, Henry!" hissed Mom.

"I CAN'T UNDERSTAND THIS MENU!" screamed Henry.

"Calm down this minute Henry," hissed Dad. "Or no $2."

Mom translated: "A tasty...uh... something on a bed of roast something with a something sauce."

"Sounds delicious," said Dad.

"Wait, there's more," said Mom. "A big piece of something enrobed with something cooked in something with carrots."

"Right, I'm having that," said Dad. "I love carrots."

Mom carried on translating. Henry opened his mouth to scream—

"Why don't you order *tripe?*" said Steve.

"What's that?" asked Henry suspiciously.

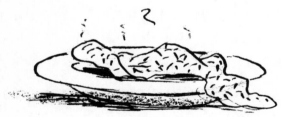

"You don't want to know," said Steve.

"Try me," said Henry.

"Intestines," said Steve. "You know, the wriggly bits in your stomach."

Horrid Henry snorted. Sometimes

he felt sorry for Steve. Did Steve really think he'd fool him with *that* old trick? *Tripe* was probably a fancy French word for spaghetti. Or cake.

"Or you could order *escargots*," said Steve. "I dare you."

"What's *escargots?*" said Henry.

Stuck-Up Steve stuck his nose in the air.

"Oh, sorry, I forgot you don't learn French at your school. *I've* been learning it for years."

"Whoopee for you," said Horrid Henry.

"*Escargots* are snails, stupid," said Stuck-Up Steve.

Steve must think he was a real idiot,

thought Horrid Henry indignantly. *Snails*. Ha ha ha. In a restaurant? As if.

"Oh yeah, right, you big fat liar," said Henry.

Steve shrugged.

"Too chicken, huh?" he sneered. "Cluck cluck cluck."

Horrid Henry was outraged. No one called him chicken and lived.

"Course not," said Horrid Henry. "I'd love to eat snails." Naturally it would turn out to be fish or something in a smelly, disgusting sauce, but so what? *Escargots* could hardly be more revolting than all the other yucky things on the menu. Steve would have to try harder than that to fool him. He would order so-called "snails" just to show Steve up for the liar he was. Then wouldn't he make fun of stupid old Steve!

"And vat are ve having tonight?" asked the French waiter.

Aunt Ruby ordered.

"An excellent choice, madame," said the waiter.

Dad ordered. The waiter kissed his fingers.

"*Magnifique*, monsieur, our speciality."

Mom ordered.

"Bravo, madame. And what about you, young man?" the waiter asked Henry.

"I'm having *escargots*," said Henry.

"Hmmm," said the waiter. "Monsieur is a gourmet?"

Horrid Henry wasn't sure he liked the sound of that. Stuck-Up Steve snickered. What was going on? thought Horrid Henry.

"Boudicca! Eat your vegetables!"

"Yes, Mom."

"Boudicca! Stop slurping."

"Yes, Mom," snapped Miss Battle-Axe.

"Boudicca! Don't pick your nose!"

"I wasn't!" said Miss Battle-Axe.

"Don't you contradict me," said Mrs. Battle-Axe.

The waiter reappeared, carrying six plates covered in silver domes.

"Voilà!" he said, whisking off the lids with a flourish. "Bon appétit!"

Everyone peered at their elegant plates.

"Ah," said Mom, looking at her squid.

44

"Ah," said Dad, looking at his stuffed tomatoes.

"Ah," said Peter, looking at his beet mousse.

Horrid Henry stared at his food. It looked like—it couldn't be—oh my gosh, it was...SNAILS! It really was snails! Squishy squashy squidgy slimy slithery slippery snails. Still in their shells.

Drenched in butter, but unmistakably
snails. Steve had tricked him.

Horrid Henry's hand reached
out to hurl the snails at Steve.

Stuck-Up Steve giggled.

Horrid Henry stopped
and gritted his teeth. No
way was he giving Steve
the satisfaction of seeing him
get into big trouble. He'd
ordered snails and he'd
eat snails. And when he
threw up, he'd make sure
it was all over Steve.

Horrid Henry grabbed
his fork and plunged. Then he
closed his eyes and popped the
snail in his mouth.

Horrid Henry chewed.

Horrid Henry chewed some
more.

"Hmmm," said Horrid Henry.

He popped another snail in his mouth. And another.

"Yummy," said Henry. "This is great." Why hadn't anyone told him that Le Posh served such thrillingly revolting food? Wait till he told Rude Ralph!

Stuck-Up Steve looked unhappy.

"How's your maggot sauce, Steve?" said Henry cheerfully.

"It's not maggot sauce," said Steve.

"Maggot maggot maggot," whispered Henry. "Watch them wriggle about."

Steve put down his fork. So did Mom, Dad, and Peter.

"Go on everyone, eat up," said Henry, chomping.

"I'm not that hungry," said Mom.

"You said we had to eat everything on our plate," said Henry.

"No I didn't," said Dad weakly.

"You did too!" said Henry. "So eat!"

"I don't like beets," moaned Perfect Peter.

"Hush, Peter," snapped Mom.

"Peter, I never thought *you* were a fussy eater," said Aunt Ruby.

"I'm not!" wailed Perfect Peter.

"Boudicca!" blasted Mrs. Battle-Axe's shrill voice. "Pay attention when I'm speaking to you!"

"Yes, Mom," said Miss Battle-Axe.

"Why can't you be as good as that boy?" said Mrs. Battle-Axe, pointing to Horrid Henry. "Look at him sitting there, eating so beautifully."

Miss Battle-Axe turned around and saw Henry. Her face went bright red, then purple, then white. She gave him a sickly smile.

Horrid Henry gave her a little polite wave. Oh boy.

For the first time in his life was he ever looking forward to school.

HORRID HENRY
GOES SHOPPING

· ·

Horrid Henry stood in his bedroom up
to his knees in clothes. The long sleeve
striped T-shirt came to his elbow. His
pants stopped halfway down his legs.
Henry sucked in his tummy as hard as
he could. Still the zipper wouldn't zip.

"Nothing fits!" he screamed, yanking
off the shirt and hurling it across the
room. "And my shoes hurt."

"All right, Henry, calm down," said
Mom. "You've grown. We'll go out
this afternoon and get you some new
clothes and shoes."

"NOOOOOOO!" shrieked Henry. "NOOOOOOOOOOOO!"

Horrid Henry hated shopping.

Correction: Horrid Henry loved shopping. He loved shopping for gigantic TVs, computer games, comics, toys, and candy. Yet for some reason Horrid Henry's parents never wanted to go shopping for good stuff. Oh no. They shopped for vacuum bags. Toothpaste. Spinach. Socks. Why oh why did he have such horrible parents? When he was grown up he'd never set foot in a

supermarket. He'd only shop for TVs, computer games, and chocolate.

But shopping for clothes was even worse than heaving his heavy bones around the Happy Shopper Supermarket. Nothing was more boring than being dragged around miles and miles and miles of shops, filled with disgusting clothes only a mutant would ever want to wear, and then standing in a little room while Mom made you try on icky scratchy things you wouldn't be seen dead in if they were the last pair of pants on earth. It was horrible enough getting dressed once a day without doing it fifty times. Just thinking about trying on shirt after shirt after shirt made Horrid Henry want to scream.

"I'm not going shopping!" he howled, kicking the pile of clothes as viciously as he could. "And you can't make me."

"What's all this yelling?" demanded Dad.

"Henry needs new pants," said Mom grimly.

Dad went pale.

"Are you sure?"

"Yes," said Mom. "Take a look at him."

Dad looked at Henry. Henry scowled.

"They're a *little* small, but not *that* bad," said Dad.

"I can't breathe in these pants!" shrieked Henry.

"That's why we're going shopping," said Mom. "And *I'll* take him." Last time Dad had taken Henry shopping for socks and came back instead with three Hairy Hellhound CDs and a jumbo pack of Day-Glo slime.

"I don't know what came over me," Dad had said when Mom told him off.

"But why do *I* have to go?" said Henry. "I don't want to waste my precious time shopping."

"What about *my* precious time?" said Mom.

Henry scowled. Parents didn't have precious time. They were there to serve their children. New pants should just magically appear, like clean clothes and packed lunches.

Mom's face brightened. "Wait, I have an idea," she beamed. She rushed out and came back with a large plastic bag.

"Here," she said, pulling out a pair of bright red pants, "try these on."

Henry looked at them suspiciously.

"Where are they from?"

"Aunt Ruby dropped off some of Steve's old clothes a few weeks ago. I'm sure we'll find something that fits you."

Horrid Henry stared at Mom. Had she gone gaga? Was she actually suggesting that he should wear his horrible cousin's moldy old shirts and smelly pants? Just imagine, putting his arms into the same stinky sleeves that Stuck-up Steve had slimed? Uggh!

"NO WAY!" screamed Henry, shuddering. "I'm not wearing Steve's smelly old clothes. I'd catch rabies."

56

"They're practically brand new," said Mom.

"I don't care," said Henry.

"But Henry," said Perfect Peter. "I always wear *your* hand-me-downs."

"So?" snarled Henry.

"I don't mind wearing hand-me-downs," said Perfect Peter. "It saves so much money. You shouldn't be so selfish, Henry."

"Quite right, Peter," said Mom, smiling. "At least *one* of my sons thinks about others."

Horrid Henry pounced. He was a vampire sampling his supper.

"AAIIIEEEEEE!" squealed Peter.

"Stop that, Henry!" screamed Mom.

"Leave your brother alone!" screamed Dad.

Horrid Henry glared at Peter.

"Peter is a worm, Peter is a toad," jeered Henry.

"Mom!" wailed Peter. "Henry said I was a worm. And a toad."

"Don't be horrid, Henry," said Dad. "Or no TV for a week. You have three choices. Wear Steve's old clothes. Wear your old clothes. Go shopping for new ones today."

"Do we *have* to go today?" moaned Henry.

"Fine," said Mom. "We'll go tomorrow."

"I don't want to go tomorrow," wailed Henry. "My weekend will be ruined."

Mom glared at Henry.

"Then we'll go right now this minute."

"NO!" screamed Horrid Henry.

"YES!" screamed Mom.

★ ★ ★

Several hours later, Mom and Henry
walked into Mellow Mall. Mom already
looked like she'd
been crossing
the Sahara desert
without water for
days. Serves her
right for bringing
me here, thought
Horrid Henry,
scowling, as he
scuffed his feet.

"Can't we go to
Shop 'n' Drop?"
whined Henry. "Graham says they've
got a win your weight in chocolate
competition."

"No," said Mom, dragging Henry into
Zippy's Department Store. "We're here
to get you some new pants and shoes.
Now hurry up, we don't have all day."

Horrid Henry looked around. Wow! There was lots of great stuff on display.

"I want the Hip-Hop Robots," said Henry.

"No," said Mom.

"I want the new Waterblaster!" screeched Henry.

"No," said Mom.

"I want a Creepy Crawly lunch box!"

"NO!" said Mom, pulling him into the boys' clothing department.

What, thought Horrid Henry grimly, is the point of going shopping if you never buy anything?

"I want Root-a-Toot sneakers with flashing red lights," said Henry. He could see himself now, strolling into class, a bugle blasting and red light flashing every time his feet hit the floor. Cool! He'd love to see Miss Battle-Axe's face when he exploded into class wearing them.

"No," said Mom, shuddering.

"Oh please," said Henry.

"NO!" said Mom, "We're here to buy pants and sensible school shoes."

"But I want Root-a-Toot sneakers!" screamed Horrid Henry. "Why can't we buy what *I* want to buy? You're the meanest mother in the world and I hate you!"

"Don't be horrid, Henry. Go and try these on," said Mom, grabbing a selection of hideous pants and revolting T-shirts. "I'll keep looking."

Horrid Henry sighed loudly and slumped toward the dressing room. No one in the world suffered as much as he did. Maybe he could hide between the clothes racks and never come out.

Then something wonderful in the toy department next door caught his eye.

Whooa! A whole row of the new megalotronic animobotic robots with 213 programmable actions. Horrid Henry dumped the clothes and ran over to have a look. Oooh, the new Intergalactic Samurai Gorillas that launched real stinkbombs! And the latest Waterblasters! And deluxe Dungeon Drink kits with a celebrity chef recipe book! To say nothing of the Mega-Whirl Goo Shooter that sprayed fluorescent goo for fifty yards in every direction. Wow!

Mom staggered into the dressing room with more clothes. "Henry?" said Mom.

No reply.

"HENRY!" said Mom.

Still no reply.

Mom yanked open a dressing room door.

"Hen—"

"Excuse *me!*" yelped a bald man, standing in his underpants.

"Sorry," said Mom, blushing bright pink. She dashed out of the changing room and scanned the shop floor.

Henry was gone.

Mom searched up the aisles.

No Henry.

Mom searched down the aisles.

Still no Henry.

Then Mom saw a tuft of hair sticking up behind the neon sign for Ballistic Bazooka Boomerangs. She marched over and hauled Henry away.

"I was just looking," protested Henry.

Henry tried on one pair of pants after another.

"No, no, no, no, no, no, no," said Henry, kicking off the final pair. "I hate all of them."

"All right," said Mom, grimly. "We'll look somewhere else."

Mom and Henry went to Top Trousers. They went to Cool Clothes. They went to Stomp in the Swamp. Nothing had been right.

"Too tight," moaned Henry.

"Too itchy!"

"Too big!"

"Too small!"

"Too ugly!"

"Too red!"

"Too uncomfortable!"

"We're going to Tip-Top Togs," said Mom wearily. "The first thing that fits, we're buying."

Mom staggered into the children's department and grabbed a pair of pink and green plaid pants in Henry's size.

"Try these on," she ordered. "If they fit we're buying them."

Horrid Henry gazed in horror at the horrendous pants.

"Those are girls' pants!" he screamed.

"They are not," said Mom.

"Are too!" shrieked Henry.

"I'm sick and tired of your excuses, Henry," said Mom. "Put them on or no allowance for a year. I mean it."

Horrid Henry put on the pink and green plaid pants, puffing out his stomach as much as possible. Not even Mom would make him buy pants that were too tight.

Oh no. The horrible pants had an elastic waist. They would fit a mouse as easily as an elephant.

"And lots of room to grow," said Mom brightly. "You can wear them for years. Perfect."

"NOOOOOO!" howled Henry. He flung himself on the floor kicking and

screaming. "NOOOO! THEY'RE GIRLS' PANTS!!!"

"We're buying them," said Mom. She gathered up the plaid pants and stomped over to the register. She tried not to think about starting all over again trying to find a pair of shoes that Henry would wear.

A little girl in pigtails walked out of the dressing room, twirling in pink and green plaid pants.

"I love them, Mommy!" she shrieked. "Let's get three pairs."

Horrid Henry stopped howling.
He looked at Mom.
Mom looked at Henry.
Then they both looked at the pink and
green plaid pants Mom was carrying.

ROOT-A-TOOT!
ROOT-A-TOOT!
ROOT-A-TOOT!
TOOT! TOOT!

An earsplitting bugle blast shook the
house. Flashing red lights bounced off
the walls.
"What's that noise?" said Dad,
covering his ears.
"What noise?" said Mom, pretending
to read.

ROOT-A-TOOT!
ROOT-A-TOOT!

ROOT-A-TOOT!
TOOT! TOOT!

Dad stared at Mom.

"You didn't," said Dad. "Not—Root-a-Toot sneakers?"

Mom hid her face in her hands.

"I don't know what came over me," said Mom.

HORRiD HENRY ROCKS

....

"Boys, I have a very special treat for you," said Mom, beaming.

Horrid Henry looked up from his *Mutant Max* comic.

Perfect Peter looked up from his spelling homework.

A treat? A special treat? A very special treat? Maybe Mom and Dad were finally appreciating him. Maybe they'd got tickets...maybe they'd actually got tickets...Horrid Henry's heart leaped. Could it be possible that at last, at long last, he'd get to go to a Killer Boy Rats concert?

"We're going to the Daffy and her Dancing Daisies show!" said Mom. "I got the last four tickets."

"OOOOOOHHHH," said Peter, clapping his hands. "Yippee! I love Daffy."

What?? NOOOOOOOOOOO! That wasn't a treat. That was torture. A treat would be a day at the Frosty Freeze Ice Cream Factory. A treat would be no school. A treat would be all he could eat at Gobble and Go.

"I don't want to see that stupid Daffy," said Horrid Henry. "I want to see the Killer Boy Rats."

"No way," said Mom.

"I don't like the Killer Boy Rats," shuddered Peter. "Too scary."

"Me neither," shuddered Mom. "Too loud."

"Me neither," shuddered Dad. "Too shouty."

"NOOOOOOOO!" screamed
Henry.

"But Henry," said Peter, "everyone
loves Daffy."

"Not me," snarled Henry.

Perfect Peter waved a flier. "Daffy's
going to be the greatest show ever.
Read this."

Daffy sings and dances her way
across the stage and into your heart.
Your chance to sing along to all your
favorite daisy songs! I'm a Lazy
Daisy. Whoops-a-Daisy. And of
course, Upsy-Daisy, Crazy Daisy,
Prance and Dance-a-Daisy.

With special guest star Busy Lizzie!!!

AAAARRRRRGGGGGHHHHHH.

Moody Margaret's parents were taking her to the Killer Boy Rats concert. Rude Ralph was going to the Killer Boy Rats concert. Even Anxious Andrew was going, and he didn't even like them. Stuck-Up Steve had been bragging for months that he was going and would be sitting in a special box. It was so unfair.

No one was a bigger Rats fan than Horrid Henry. Henry had all their albums: *Killer Boy Rats Attack-Tack-Tack*, *Killer Boy Rats Splat!*, *Killer Boy Rats Manic Panic*.

"It's not fair!" screamed Horrid Henry. "I want to see the Killers!!!!"

76

"We have to see something that everyone in the family will like," said Mom. "Peter's too young for the Killer Boy Rats but we can all enjoy Daffy."

"Not me!" screamed Henry.

Oh, why did he have such a stupid diaper baby for a brother? Younger brothers should be banned. They just wrecked everything. When he was King Henry the Horrible, all younger brothers would be arrested and dumped in a volcano.

In fact, why wait?

Horrid Henry pounced. He was a fiery god scooping up a human sacrifice and hurling him into the volcano's molten depths.

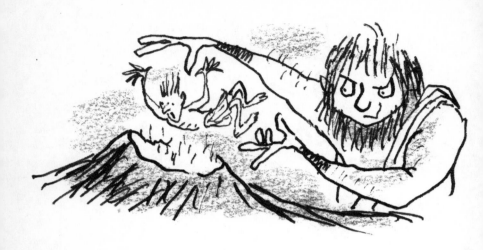

"AAAIIIIIEEEEEEE!" screamed
Perfect Peter. "Henry attacked me."

"Stop being horrid, Henry!" shouted
Mom. "Leave your brother alone."

"I won't go to Daffy," yelled Henry.
"And you can't make me."

"Go to your room," said Dad.

Horrid Henry paced up and down his
bedroom, singing his favorite Rats song
at the top of his lungs:

**"I'm dead, you're dead, we're dead.
Get over it.
Dead is great, dead's where it's at
'Cause..."**

"Henry! Be quiet!" screamed Dad.

"I am being quiet!" bellowed Henry.
Honestly. Now, how could he get out
of going to that terrible Daffy concert?
He'd easily be the oldest one there.
Only stupid babies liked Daffy. If the
horrible songs didn't kill him then he
was sure to die of embarrassment. Then
they'd be sorry they'd made him go.
But it would be too late. Mom and Dad
and Peter could sob and boohoo all they
liked but he'd still be dead. And serve
them right for being so mean to him.

Dad said if he was good he could see
the Killer Boys next time they were
in town. Ha. The Killer Boy Rats
NEVER put on concerts. Next time

they did he'd be old and hobbling and whacking Peter with his cane.

He had to get a Killer Boys ticket now. He just had to. But how? They'd been sold out for weeks.

Maybe he could place an ad:

Can you help?
Deserving boy suffering from rare and terrible illness. His ears are falling off. Doctor has prescribed the Killer Boy Rats cure. Only by hearing the Rats live is there any hope. If you've got a ticket to the concert on Saturday PLEASE send it to Henry NOW. (If you don't you know you'll be sorry.)

That might work. Or he could tell
people that the concert was cursed and
anyone who went would turn into a
rat. Hmmm. Somehow Henry didn't
see Margaret falling for that. Too bad
Peter didn't have a ticket, thought
Henry sadly, he could tell him he'd turn
into a killer and Peter would hand over
the ticket instantly.

And then suddenly Horrid Henry
had a brilliant, spectacular idea. There
must be someone out there who was
desperate for a Daffy ticket. In fact there
must be someone out there who would
swap a Killers ticket for a Daffy one. It
was certainly worth a try.

"Hey, Brian, I hear you've got a Killer
Boy Rats ticket," said Horrid Henry at
school the next day.

"So?" said Brainy Brian.

"I've got a ticket to something much
better," said Henry.

"What?" said Brian. "The Killers are
the best."

Horrid Henry could barely force
the grisly words out of his mouth. He
twisted his lips into a smile.

"Daffy and her Dancing Daisies," said
Horrid Henry.

Brainy Brian stared at him.

"Daffy and her Dancing Daisies?" he spluttered.

"Yes," said Horrid Henry brightly. "I've heard it's their best show ever. Great new songs. You'd love it. Wanna swap?"

Brainy Brian stared at him as if he had a turnip instead of a head.

"You're trying to swap Daffy and her Dancing Daisies tickets for the Killer Boy Rats?" said Brian slowly.

"I'm doing you a favor, no one likes the Killer Boy Rats anymore," said Henry.

"I do," said Brian.

Rats.

"How come you have a ticket for Daffy?" said Brian. "Isn't that a baby show?"

"It's not mine, I found it," said Horrid Henry quickly. Oops.

"Ha ha, Henry, I'm seeing the Killers, and you're not," Margaret taunted.

"Yeah, Henry," said Sour Susan.

"I heard…" Margaret doubled over laughing, "I heard you were going to the Daffy show!"

"That's a big fat lie," said Henry hotly. "I wouldn't be seen dead there."

Horrid Henry looked around the auditorium at the sea of little baby nappy faces. There was Needy Neil clutching his mother's hand. There was Weepy William, crying because he'd dropped his ice cream. There was Toddler Tom, up past his bedtime. Oh, no! There was Lisping Lily. Henry ducked.

Phew. She hadn't seen him. Margaret would never stop teasing him if she ever found out. When he was king, Daffy and her Dancing Daisies would live in a dungeon with only rats for company. Anyone who so much as mentioned the name Daffy, or even grew a daisy, would be flushed down the toilet.

There was a round of polite applause as Daffy and her Dancing Daisies pirouetted on stage. Horrid Henry slumped in his seat as far as he could slump and pulled his cap over his face. Thank goodness he'd come disguised

and brought some earplugs. No one
would ever know he'd been there.

"Tra la la la la la la!" trilled the Daisies.

"Tra la la la la la la!" trilled the
audience.

Oh, the torture, groaned Horrid
Henry as horrible song followed
horrible song. Perfect Peter sang along.
So did Mom and Dad.

AAARRRRRGGGHHHHH. And

to think that tomorrow night the Killer Boy Rats would be performing…and he wouldn't be there! It was so unfair.

Then Daffy cartwheeled to the front of the stage. One of the daisies stood beside her holding a giant hat.

"And now the moment all you Daffy Daisy fans have been waiting for," squealed Daffy. "It's the Lucky Ducky Daisy Draw, when we call up on stage an oh-so-lucky audience member to lead us in the Whoops-a-Daisy sing-along song! Who's it going to be?"

"Me!" squealed Peter. Mom squeezed his arm.

Daffy fumbled in the hat and pulled out a ticket.

"And the lucky winner of our ticket raffle is…Henry! Ticket 597! Ticket 597, yes, Henry, you in row P, seat 10, come on up! Daffy needs you on stage!"

Horrid Henry was stuck to his seat in horror. It must be some other Henry. Never in his worst nightmares had he ever imagined—

"Henry, that's you," said Perfect Peter. "You're so lucky."

"Henry! Come on up, Henry!" shrieked Daffy. "Don't be shy!"

Onstage at the Daffy show? No! No!

Wait till Moody Margaret found out.
Wait till anyone found out. Henry would
never hear the end of it. He wasn't
moving. Pigs would fly before he budged.

"Henwy!" squealed Lisping Lily
behind him. "Henwy! I want to give
you a big kiss, Henwy…"

Horrid Henry leaped out of his
seat. Lily! Lisping Lily! That fiend in
toddler's clothing would stop at nothing
to get hold of him.

Before Henry knew what had happened, ushers dressed as daisies had nabbed him and pushed him onstage.

Horrid Henry blinked in the lights. Was anyone in the world as unlucky as he?

"All together now, everyone get ready to ruffle their petals. Let's sing Tippy-toe daisy do/Let us sing a song for you!" beamed Daffy. "Henry, you start us off."

Horrid Henry stared at the vast audience. Everyone was looking at him. Of course he didn't know any stupid Daisy songs. He always blocked his ears or ran from the room whenever Peter sang them. Whatever could the words be…"Watch out, whoop-de-do/Daisy's doing a big poo?"

These poor stupid kids. If only they could hear some decent songs, like… like…

**"Granny on her crutches
Push her off her chair
Shove Shove Shove Shove
Shove her down the stairs."**

shrieked Horrid Henry.

The audience was silent. Daffy looked stunned.

"Uh, Henry…that's not Tippy-toe daisy do," whispered Daffy.

"C'mon everyone, join in with me," shouted Horrid Henry, spinning around and twirling in his best Killer Boy Rats manner.

**"I'M iN my coffin
No time for coughin'
wheN you're squished dowN dead.
DoN't care if you're a goony
DoN't care if you're a loony,
DoN't care if you're cartooNy
I'll squish you!"**

sang Horrid Henry as loud as he could.

**"GonNa be a rock star (aNd you ain't)
DoN't even—"**

Two security guards ran onstage and grabbed Horrid Henry.

"Killer Boy Rats forever!" shrieked Henry as he was dragged off.

Horrid Henry stared at the special
delivery letter covered in skulls and
crossbones. His hand shook.

Hey Henry,
We saw a video of you singing our
songs and getting yanked off stage—
way to go killer boy! Here's a pair of
tickets for our concert tonight, and a
backstage pass—see you there.
The Killer Boy Rats

Horrid Henry goggled at the tickets and the backstage pass. He couldn't move. He couldn't breathe. He was going to the Killer Boy Rats concert. He was actually going to the Killer Boy Rats concert.

Life, thought Horrid Henry, beaming, was sweet.

HORRiD HENRY'S HORRiD WEEKEND

....

"NOOOOOOOOO!" screamed Horrid Henry. "I don't want to spend the weekend with Steve."

"Don't be horrid, Henry," said Mom. "It's very kind of Aunt Ruby to invite us down for the weekend."

"But I hate Aunt Ruby!" shrieked Henry. "And I hate Steve and I hate you!"

"I can't wait to go," said Perfect Peter.

"Shut up, Peter!" howled Henry.

"Don't tell your brother to shut up," shouted Mom.

"Shut up! Shut up! Shut up!" And

Horrid Henry fell to the floor wailing
and screaming and kicking.

Stuck-Up Steve was Horrid Henry's
hideous cousin. Steve hated Henry.
Henry hated him. The last time Henry
had seen Steve, Henry had tricked
him into thinking there was a monster
under his bed. Steve had sworn
revenge. Then there was the other time
at the restaurant when…well, Horrid
Henry thought it would be a good idea
to avoid Steve until his cousin was
grown-up and in prison for crimes
against humanity.

And now his mean, horrible parents were forcing him to spend a whole precious weekend with the toadiest, wormiest, smelliest boy who ever slimed out of a swamp.

Mom sighed. "We're going and that's that. Ruby says Steve is having a lovely friend over so that should be extra fun."

Henry stopped screaming and kicking. Maybe Steve's friend wouldn't be a stuck-up monster. Maybe *he'd* been forced to waste his weekend with Steve too. After all, who'd volunteer to spend time with Steve? Maybe together they could squish Stuck-Up Steve once and for all.

Ding dong.

Horrid Henry, Perfect Peter, Mom, and Dad stood outside Rich Aunt Ruby's enormous house on a gray, drizzly day. Steve opened the massive front door.

"Oh," he sneered. "It's you."

Steve opened the present Mom had brought. It was a small flashlight. Steve put it down.

"I already have a much better one," he said.

"Oh," said Mom.

Another boy stood beside him. A boy who looked vaguely familiar. A boy... Horrid Henry gasped. Oh no. It was Bill. Bossy Bill. The horrible son of Dad's boss. Henry had once tricked Bill into photocopying his bottom. Bill had sworn revenge. Horrid Henry's insides turned to jelly. Trust Stuck-Up Steve to be friends with Bossy Bill. It was bad enough being trapped in a house with one archenemy. Now he was stuck in a house with *two*...

Stuck-Up Steve scowled at Henry. "You're wearing that old shirt of mine," he said. "Don't your parents ever buy you new clothes?"

Bossy Bill snorted.

"Steve," said Aunt Ruby. "Don't be rude."

"I wasn't," said Steve. "I was just asking. No harm in asking, is there?"

"No," said Horrid Henry. He smiled at Steve. "So when will Aunt Ruby buy you a new face?"

"Henry," said Mom. "Don't be rude."

101

"I was just asking," said Henry. "No harm in asking, is there?" he added, glaring at Steve.

Steve glared back.

Aunt Ruby beamed. "Henry, Steve and Bill are taking you to their friend Tim's paintballing party."

"Won't that be fun," said Mom.

Peter looked frightened.

"Don't worry, Peter," said Aunt Ruby, "you can help me plant seedlings while the older boys are out."

Peter beamed. "Thank you," he said. "I don't like paintballing. Too messy and scary."

Paintballing! Horrid Henry loved paintballing. The chance to splat Steve and Bill with ooey gooey globs of paint...hmmm, maybe the weekend was looking up.

"Great!" said Horrid Henry.

"How nice," said Rich Aunt Ruby,
"you boys already know each other.
Think how much fun you're all going to
have sharing Steve's bedroom together."

Uh-oh, thought Horrid Henry.

"Yeah!" said Stuck-Up Steve. "We're
looking forward to sharing a room with
Henry." His piggy eyes gleamed.

"Yeah!" said Bossy Bill. "I can't
wait." His piggy eyes gleamed.

"Yeah," said Horrid Henry. He wouldn't be sleeping a wink.

Horrid Henry looked around the enormous high-ceilinged bedroom he'd be sharing with his two evil enemies for two very long days and one very long night. There was a bunk bed, which Steve and Bill had already nabbed, and two single beds. Steve's bedroom shelves were stuffed with zillions of new toys and games, as usual.

Bill and Steve smirked at each other. Henry scowled at them. What were they plotting?

"Don't you dare touch my Super-Blooper Blaster," said Steve.

"Don't you dare touch my Demon Dagger Saber," said Bill.

A Super-Blooper Blaster! A Demon Dagger Saber! Trust Bill and Steve to have the two best toys in the world…Rats.

"Don't worry," said Henry. "I don't play with baby toys."

"Oh yeah," said Stuck-Up Steve. "Bet you're too much of a baby to jump off my top bunk onto your bed."

"Am not," said Henry.

"We're not allowed to jump on beds," said Perfect Peter.

"We're not allowed," mimicked Steve. "I thought you were too poor to even *have* beds."

"Ha ha," said Henry.

"Chicken. Chicken. Scaredy-cat," sneered Bossy Bill.

"Squawk!" said Stuck-Up Steve. "I knew you'd be too scared, chicken."

That did it. *No* one called Horrid Henry chicken and lived. As if he, Henry, leader of a pirate gang, would be afraid to jump off a top bunk. Ha.

"Don't do it, Henry," said Perfect Peter.

"Shut up, worm," said Henry.

"But it's so high," squealed Peter, squeezing his eyes shut.

Horrid Henry clambered up the ladder and stepped onto the top bunk. "It's nothing," he lied. "I've jumped off *much* higher."

"Well, go on then," said Stuck-Up Steve.

Boing! Horrid Henry bounced.

Boing! Horrid Henry bounced higher. Whee! This bed was very springy.

"We're waiting, chicken," said Bossy Bill.

BOING! BOING! Horrid Henry bent his knees, then—leap! He jumped onto the single bed below.

SMASH!

Horrid Henry crashed to the floor as the bed collapsed beneath him.

Huh? What? How could he have broken the bed? He hadn't heard any breaking sounds. It was as if…as if…

Mom, Dad, and Aunt Ruby ran into the room.

"Henry broke the bed," said Stuck-Up Steve.

"We tried to stop him," said Bossy Bill, "but Henry insisted on jumping."

"But...but..." said Horrid Henry.

"Henry!" wailed Mom. "You horrid boy."

"How could you be so horrid?" said Dad. "No allowance for a year. Ruby, I'm so sorry."

Aunt Ruby pursed her lips. "These things happen," she said.

"And no paintballing party for you," said Mom.

What?

"No!" wailed Henry.

Then Horrid Henry saw a horrible sight. Behind Aunt Ruby's back, Steve and Bill were covering their mouths and laughing. Henry realized the terrible truth. Bill and Steve had tricked him. *They'd* broken the bed. And now *he'd* gotten the blame.

"But I didn't break it!" screamed Henry.

"Yes you did, Henry," said Peter. "I saw you."

AAAARRRRGGGGHHHH! Horrid Henry leaped at Peter. He was a storm god hurling thunderbolts at a foolish mortal.

"AAAIIIEEEEEE!" squealed Perfect Peter.

"Henry! Stop it!" shrieked Mom. "Leave your brother alone."

Nah nah ne nah nah mouthed Steve behind Aunt Ruby's back.

"Isn't it lovely how nicely the boys are playing together?" said Aunt Ruby.

"Yes, isn't it?" said Mom.

"Not surprising," said Aunt Ruby, beaming. "After all, Steve is such a polite, friendly boy, I've never met anyone who didn't love him."

Snore! Snore! Snore!

Horrid Henry lay on a mattress listening to hideous snoring sounds. He'd stayed awake for hours, just in case they tried anything horrible, like pouring water on his head, or stuffing frogs in his bed. Which was what he was going to do to Peter, the moment he got home.

Henry had just spent the most horrible Saturday of his life. He'd begged to go to the paintballing party. He'd pleaded to go to the paintballing party. He'd screamed about going to the paintballing party. But no. His mean, horrible parents wouldn't budge. And it was all Steve and Bill's fault. They'd tripped him going down the stairs.

They'd kicked him under the table at lunch (and then complained that he was kicking *them*). And every time Aunt

Ruby's back was turned they stuck out their tongues and jeered: "We're going paintballing and you're not."

He had to get to that party. And he had to be revenged. But how? How? His two archenemies had banded together and struck the first blow. Could he booby-trap their beds and remove a few slats? Unfortunately, everyone would know *he'd* done it and he'd be in even more trouble than he was now.

Scare them? Tell them there was a monster under the bed? Hmmm. He knew Steve was as big a scaredy-cat as Peter. But he'd already done that once. He didn't think Steve would fall for it again.

Get them into trouble? Turn them against each other? Steal their best toys and hide them? Hmmm. Hmmm.

Horrid Henry thought and thought.
He had to be revenged. He had to.

Tweet tweet. It was Sunday morning.
The birds were singing. The sun was
shining. The—

Yank!

Bossy Bill and Stuck-Up Steve pulled
off his blanket.

"Nah na ne nah nah, we-ee beat
you," crowed Bill.

"Nah na ne nah nah, we got you into
trouble," crowed Steve.

Horrid Henry scowled. Time to put
Operation Revenge into action.

"Bill thinks you're bossy, Steve," said
Henry. "He told me."

"Did not," said Bossy Bill.

"And Steve thinks you're stuck-up,
Bill," added Henry sweetly.

"No, I don't," said Steve.

"Then why'd you tell me that?" said
Horrid Henry.

Steve stuck his nose in the air. "Nice
try, Henry, you big loser," said Stuck-Up
Steve. "Just ignore him, Bill."

"Henry, it's not nice to tell lies," said
Perfect Peter.

"Shut up, worm," snarled Horrid Henry.
Rats.

Time for plan B.

Except he didn't have a plan B.

"I can't wait for Tim's party," said Bossy
Bill. "You never know what's going to
happen."

"Yeah, remember when he told us he
was having a pirate party and instead we
went to the Wild West Theme Park!"
said Steve.

"Or when he said we were having a
sleepover, and instead we all went to a
Manic Buzzards concert."

"And Tim gives the best party bags.
Last year everyone got a Deluxe
Demon Dagger Saber," said Steve.
"Wonder what he'll give this year?
Oh, I forgot, Henry won't be coming
to the party."

"Too bad you can't come, Henry,"
sneered Bossy Bill.

"Yeah, too bad," sneered Stuck-Up
Steve. "Not."

ARRRRGGGHH. Horrid Henry's
blood boiled. He couldn't decide what
was worse, listening to them crow
about having gotten him into so much
trouble or brag about the great party
they were going to and he wasn't.

"I can't wait to find out what surprises
he'll have in store this year," said Bill.

"Yeah," said Steve.

Who cares? thought Horrid Henry.
Unless Tim was planning to throw Bill

and Steve into a shark tank. That would
be a nice surprise. Unless of course…

And then suddenly Horrid Henry had a brilliant, spectacular idea. It was so brilliant and so spectacular, that for a moment he wondered whether he could stop himself from flinging open the window and shouting his plan out loud. Oh wow. Oh wow. It was risky. It was dangerous. But if it worked, he would have the best revenge ever in the history of the world. No, the history of the solar system. No, the history of the universe!

It was an hour before the party. Horrid Henry was counting the seconds until he could escape.

Aunt Ruby popped her head around the door waving an envelope.

"Letter for you boys," she said.

Steve snatched it and tore it open.

Dear Steve and Bill
Party of the year update.
Everyone must come to my house
wearing pajamas (You'll find
out why later, but don't be
surprised if we all end up in
a movie — shhhh). It'll be a real
laugh. Make sure to bring
your favorite soft toys too,
and wear your fluffiest
slippers. Hollywood, here
we come!

Tim

"He must be planning something
amazing," said Bill.

"I bet we're all going to be acting in a
movie!" said Steve.

"Yeah!" said Bill.

"Too bad *you* won't, Henry," said Stuck-Up Steve.

"You're so lucky," said Henry. "I wish I were going."

Mom looked at Dad.

Dad looked at Mom.

Henry held his breath.

"Well, you can't, Henry, and that's final," said Mom.

"It's so unfair!" shrieked Henry.

Henry's parents dropped Steve and Bill off at Tim's party on their way home. Steve was in his blue bunny pajamas and blue bunny fluffy slippers and clutching a panda.

Bill was in his yellow duckling pajamas and yellow duckling fluffy slippers and clutching his monkey.

"Shame you can't come, Henry," said

Steve, smirking. "But we'll be sure to tell you all about it."

"Do," said Henry as Mom drove off.

Horrid Henry heard squeals of laughter at Hoity-Toity Tim's front door. Bill and Steve stood frozen. Then they started to wave frantically at the car.

"Are they saying something?" said Mom, glancing in the rearview mirror.

"Nah, just waving good-bye," said Horrid Henry. He rolled down his window.

"Have fun, guys!"

HORRID HENRY'S
CAR JOURNEY

. . . .

"Henry! We're waiting!"

"Henry! Get down here!"

"Henry! I'm warning you!"

Horrid Henry sat on his bed and scowled. His mean, horrible parents could warn him all they liked. He wasn't moving.

"Henry! We're going to be late," yelled Mom.

"Good!" shouted Henry.

"Henry! This is your final warning," yelled Dad.

"I don't want to go to Polly's!"

screamed Henry. "I want to go to Ralph's birthday party."

Mom stomped upstairs.

"Well you can't," said Mom. "You're coming to the christening, and that's that."

"NO!" screeched Henry. "I hate Polly, I hate babies, and I hate you!"

Henry had been a ring bearer at the wedding of his cousin, Prissy Polly, when she'd married Pimply Paul. Now they had a prissy, pimply baby, Vomiting Vera.

Henry had met Vera once before. She'd thrown up all over him. Henry had hoped never to see her again until she was grown up and behind bars, but no such luck. He had to go and watch her be dunked in a vat of water, on the same day that Ralph was having a birthday party at Goo-Shooter World. Henry had been longing for ages to go to Goo-Shooter World. Today was his chance. His only chance. But no. Everything was ruined.

Perfect Peter poked his head around the door.

"I'm all ready, Mom," said Perfect Peter. His shoes were polished, his teeth were brushed, and his hair neatly combed. "I know how annoying it is to be kept waiting when you're in a rush."

"Thank you, darling Peter," said Mom. "At least one of my children knows how to behave."

Horrid Henry roared and attacked. He was a swooping vulture digging his claws into a dead mouse.

"AAAAAAAAAEEEEE!" squealed
Peter.

"Stop being horrid, Henry!" said Mom.

"No one told me it was today!"
screeched Henry.

"Yes we did," said Mom. "But you
weren't paying attention."

"As usual," said Dad.

"I knew we were going," said Peter.

"I DON'T WANT TO GO TO
POLLY'S!" screamed Henry. "I want
to go to Ralph's!"

"Get in the car—NOW!" said Dad.

"Or no TV for a year!" said Mom.

Eeek! Horrid Henry stopped wailing.
No TV for a year. Anything was better
than that.

Grimly, he stomped down the stairs
and out the front door. They wanted
him in the car. They'd have him in
the car.

"Don't slam the door," said Mom.
SLAM!

Horrid Henry pushed Peter away from
the car door and scrambled for the left-
hand side behind the driver. Perfect
Peter grabbed his legs and tried to
climb over him.

Victory! Henry got there first.

Henry liked sitting on the left-hand side so he could watch the speedometer.

Peter liked sitting on the left-hand side so he could watch the speedometer.

"Mom," said Peter. "It's my turn to sit on the left!"

"No it isn't," said Henry. "It's mine."

"Mine!"

"Mine!"

"We haven't even left and already you're fighting?" said Dad.

"You'll take turns," said Mom. "You can switch after we stop."

Vroom. Vroom.

Dad started the car.

The doors locked.

Horrid Henry was trapped.

But wait. Was there a glimmer of hope? Was there a teeny tiny chance?

What was it Mom always said when he and Peter were squabbling in the car? "If you don't stop fighting I'm going to turn around and go home!" And wasn't home just exactly where he wanted to be? All he had to do was to do what he did best.

"Could I have a story CD please?" said Perfect Peter.

"No! I want a music CD," said Horrid Henry.

"I want 'Mouse Goes to Town'," said Peter.

"I want 'Driller Cannibals' Greatest Hits'," said Henry.

"Story!"

"Music!"

"Story!"

"Music!"

SMACK!

SMACK!

"Waaaaaa!"

"Stop it, Henry," said Mom.

"Tell Peter to leave me alone!" screamed Henry.

"Tell Henry to leave *me* alone!" screamed Peter.

"Leave each other alone," said Mom. Horrid Henry glared at Perfect Peter. Perfect Peter glared at Horrid Henry. Horrid Henry stretched. Slowly, steadily, centimeter by centimeter, he spread out into Peter's area.

"Henry's on my side!"

"No I'm not!"

"Henry, leave Peter alone," said Dad. "I mean it."

"I'm not doing anything," said Henry. "Are we there yet?"

"No," said Dad.

Thirty seconds passed.

"Are we there yet?" said Horrid Henry.

"No!" said Mom.

"Are we there yet?" said Horrid Henry.

"NO!" screamed Mom and Dad.

"We only left ten minutes ago," said Dad.

Ten minutes! Horrid Henry felt as if they'd been traveling for hours.

"Are we a quarter of the way there yet?"

"NO!"

"Are we halfway there yet?"

"NO!!"

"How much longer until we're halfway there?"

"Stop it, Henry!" screamed Mom.

"You're driving me crazy!" screamed Dad. "Now be quiet and leave us alone."

Henry sighed. Boy, was this boring. Why didn't they have a decent car, with built-in video games, movies, and jacuzzi? That's just what he'd have, when he was king.

Softly, he started to hum under his breath.

"Henry's humming!"

"Stop being horrid, Henry!"

"I'm not doing anything," protested Henry. He lifted his foot.

"MOM!" squealed Peter. "Henry's kicking me."

"Are you kicking him, Henry?"

"Not yet," muttered Henry. Then he screamed.

"Mom! Peter's looking out of my window!"

"Dad! Henry's looking out of *my* window."

"Peter breathed on me."

"Henry's breathing loud on purpose."

"Henry's staring at me."

"Peter's on my side!"

"Tell him to stop!" screamed Henry and Peter.

Mom's face was red.

Dad's face was red.

"That's it!" screamed Dad.

"I can't take this anymore!" screamed Mom.

Yes! thought Henry. We're going to turn back!

But instead of turning around, the car screeched to a halt at a gas station.

"We're going to take a break," said Mom. She looked exhausted.

"Who needs to pee?" said Dad. He looked even worse.

"Me," said Peter.

"Henry?"

"No," said Henry. He wasn't a baby.

He knew when he needed to pee and he didn't need to now.

"This is our only stop, Henry," said Mom. "I think you should go."

"NO!" screamed Henry. Several people looked up. "I'll wait in the car."

Mom and Dad were too tired to argue. They disappeared into the station with Peter.

Rats. Despite his best efforts, it looked like Mom and Dad were going to carry on. Well, if he couldn't make them turn back, maybe he could *delay* them? Somehow? Suddenly Henry had a wonderful, spectacular idea. It couldn't be easier, and it was guaranteed to work. He'd miss the christening!

Mom, Dad, and Peter got back in the car. Mom drove off.

"I need to pee," said Henry.

"Not now, Henry."

"I NEED TO PEE!" screamed Henry. "NOW!"

Mom headed back to the gas station.

Dad and Henry went to the restroom.

"I'll wait for you outside," said Dad. "Hurry up or we'll be late."

Late! What a lovely word.

Henry went into the restroom and locked the door. Then he waited. And waited. And waited.

Finally, he heard Dad's grumpy voice.

"Henry? Have you fallen in?"

Henry rattled the door.

"I'm locked in," said Henry. "The door's stuck. I can't get out."

"Try, Henry," pleaded Dad.

"I have," said Henry. "I guess they'll have to break the door down."

That should take a few hours. He settled himself on the toilet seat and got out a comic.

"Or you could just crawl underneath the partition into the next stall," said Dad.

Aaargghh. Henry could have burst into tears. Wasn't it just his rotten luck to try to get locked in a restroom that had gaps on the sides? Henry didn't really want to be wriggling around on the cold floor. Sighing, he gave the stall door a tug and opened it.

Horrid Henry sat in silence for the rest of the trip. He was so depressed he didn't even protest when Peter demanded his turn on the left. Plus, he felt car sick.

Henry rolled down his window.

"Mom!" said Peter. "I'm cold."

Dad turned the heat on.

"Having the heat on makes me feel sick," said Henry.

"I'm going to be sick!" whimpered Peter.

"I'm going to be sick," whined Henry.

"But we're almost there," screeched Mom. "Can't you hold on until—"

Bleeeechh.

Peter threw up all over Mom.

Bleeeechhh. Henry threw up all over Dad.

The car pulled into the driveway.

Mom and Dad staggered out of the car to Polly's front door.

"We survived," said Mom, mopping her dress.

"Thank God that's over," said Dad, mopping his shirt.

Horrid Henry scuffed

his feet sadly behind them. Despite all his hard work, he'd lost the battle. While Rude Ralph and Dizzy Dave and Jolly Josh were dashing around spraying each other with green goo later this afternoon he'd be stuck at a boring party with lots of grown-ups yak yak yaking. Oh misery!

Ding dong.

The door opened. It was Prissy Polly. She was in her bathrobe and slippers. She carried a stinky, smelly, wailing baby over her shoulder. Pimply Paul followed. He was wearing a filthy T-shirt with vomit down the front.

"Eeeek," squeaked Polly.

Mom tried to look as if she had not been through hell and barely lived to tell the tale.

"We're here!" said Mom brightly. "How's the lovely baby?"

"Too prissy," said Polly.

"Too pimply," said Paul.

Polly and Paul looked at Mom and Dad.

"What are you doing here?" said Polly finally.

"We're here for the christening," said Mom.

"Vera's christening?" said Polly.

"It's next weekend," said Paul.

Mom looked like she wanted to sag to the floor.

Dad looked like he wanted to sag beside her.

"We've come on the wrong day?" whispered Mom.

"You mean, we have to go and come back?" whispered Dad.

"Yes," said Polly.

"Oh no," said Mom.

"Oh no," said Dad.

"Bleeech," vomited Vera.

"Eeeek!" wailed Polly. "Gotta go."
She slammed the door.

"You mean, we can go home?" said Henry. "Now?"

"Yes," whispered Mom.

"Whoopee!" screamed Henry. "Hang on, Ralph, here I come!"

HORRID HENRY'S HIKE

. . . .

Horrid Henry looked out the window.
AAARRRGGGHHH! It was a
beautiful day. The sun was shining. The
birds were tweeting. The breeze was
blowing. Little fluffy clouds floated by
in a bright blue sky.

Rats.

Why couldn't it be raining? Or
hailing? Or sleeting?

Any minute, any second, it would
happen…the words he'd been dreading,
the words he'd give anything not to
hear, the words—

"Henry! Peter! Time to go for a walk," called Mom.

"Yippee!" said Perfect Peter. "I can wear my new yellow boots!"

"NO!" screamed Horrid Henry.

Go for a walk! Go for a walk! Didn't he walk enough already? He walked to school. He walked home

from school. He walked to the TV. He walked to the computer. He walked to the candy jar *and* all the way back to the comfy black chair.

Horrid Henry walked plenty. Ugghh.
The last thing he needed was more
walking. More chocolate, yes. More
chips, yes. More *walking?* No way!
Why oh why couldn't his parents ever
say, "Henry! Time to play on the
computer." Or "Henry, stop doing
your homework this minute! Time to
turn on the TV."

But no. For some reason his mean,
horrible parents thought he spent too
much time sitting indoors. They'd been
threatening for weeks to make him go
on a family walk. Now the dreadful
moment had come. His precious
weekend was ruined.

Horrid Henry hated nature. Horrid
Henry hated fresh air. What could be
more boring than walking up and down
streets staring at lampposts? Or sloshing
across some stupid muddy park? Nature

smelled. Uggh! He'd much rather be inside watching TV.

Mom stomped into the living room.

"Henry! Didn't you hear me calling?"

"No," lied Henry.

"Get your boots on, we're going," said Dad, rubbing his hands. "What a lovely day."

"I don't want to go for a walk," said Henry. "I want to watch *Rapper Zapper Zaps Terminator Gladiator.*"

"But Henry," said Perfect Peter, "fresh air and exercise are so good for you."

"I don't care!" shrieked Henry.

Horrid Henry stomped downstairs and flung open the front door. He breathed in deeply, hopped on one foot, then shut the door.

"There! Done it. Fresh air *and* exercise," snarled Henry.

"Henry, we're going," said Mom. "Get in the car."

Henry's ears pricked up.

"The car?" said Henry. "I thought we were going for a walk."

"We are," said Mom. "In the countryside."

"Hurray!" said Perfect Peter. "A nice *long* walk."

"NOOOO!" howled Henry. Plodding along in the boring old park was bad enough, with its moldy leaves and dog poo and stumpy trees. But at least the park wasn't very big. But the *countryside?*

The countryside was enormous! They'd be walking for hours, days, weeks, months, till his legs wore down to stumps and his feet fell off. And the countryside was so dangerous! Horrid Henry was sure he'd be swallowed up

by quicksand or trampled to death by marauding chickens.

"I live in the city!" shrieked Henry. "I don't want to go to the country!"

"Time you got out more," said Dad.

"But look at those clouds," moaned Henry, pointing to a fluffy wisp. "We'll get soaked."

"A little water never hurt anyone," said Mom.

Oh yeah? Wouldn't they be sorry when he died of pneumonia.

"I'm staying here and that's final!" screamed Henry.

"Henry, we're waiting," said Mom.

"Good," said Henry.

"*I'm* all ready, Mom," said Peter.

"I'm going to start deducting money from your allowance," said Dad. "Five cents, ten cents, fifteen cents, twenty—"

Horrid Henry pulled on his boots, stomped out the door, and got in the car. He slammed the door as hard as he could. It was so unfair! Why did he never get to do what *he* wanted to do? Now he would miss the first time Rapper Zapper had ever slugged it out with Terminator Gladiator. And all because he had to go on a long, boring, exhausting, horrible hike. He was so miserable he didn't even have the energy to kick Peter.

"Can't we just walk around the block?" moaned Henry.

"N-O spells no," said Dad. "We're

going for a nice walk in the countryside and that's that."

Horrid Henry slumped miserably in his seat. Boy would they be sorry when he was gobbled up by goats. Boo hoo, if only we hadn't gone on that walk in the wild, Mom would wail.

Henry was right, we should have listened to him, Dad would sob. I miss Henry, Peter would howl. I'll never eat goat's cheese again. And now it's too late, they would shriek.

If only, thought Horrid Henry. That would serve them right.

All too soon, Mom pulled into a parking lot, on the edge of a small forest.

"Wow," said Perfect Peter. "Look at all those pretty trees."

"Bet there are werewolves hiding there," muttered Henry. "And I hope they come and eat *you!*"

"Mom!" squealed Peter. "Henry's trying to scare me."

"Don't be horrid, Henry," said Mom.

Horrid Henry looked around him. There was a gate, leading to endless meadows bordered by bushes. A muddy path wound through the trees and across the fields. A church spire stuck up in the distance.

"All right, I've seen the countryside, let's go home," said Henry.

Mom glared at him.

"What?" said Henry, scowling.

"Let's enjoy this lovely day," said Dad, sighing.

"So what do we do now?" said Henry.

"Walk," said Dad.

"Where?" said Henry.

"Just walk," said Mom, "and enjoy the beautiful scenery."

Henry groaned.

"We're heading for the lake," said Dad, striding off. "I've brought bread and we can feed the ducks."

"But *Rapper Zapper* starts in an hour!"

"Tough," said Mom.

Mom, Dad, and Peter headed through the gate into the field. Horrid Henry trailed behind them walking as slowly as he could.

"Ahh, breathe the lovely fresh air," said Mom.

"We should do this more often," said Dad.

Henry sniffed.

The horrible smell of manure filled his nostrils.

"Ewww, smelly," said Henry. "Peter, couldn't you wait?"

"MOM!" shrieked Peter. "Henry called me smelly."

"Did not!"

"Did too!"

"Did not, smelly."

"WAAAAAAAAA!" wailed Peter. "Tell him to stop!"

"Don't be horrid, Henry!" screamed Mom. Her voice echoed. A dog walker passed her and glared.

"Peter, would you rather run a mile, jump a fence, or eat a country pancake?" said Henry sweetly.

"Ooh," said Peter. "I love pancakes. And a country one must be even more delicious than a city one."

"Ha ha," cackled Horrid Henry,

sticking out his tongue. "Fooled you. Peter wants to eat cow pies!"

"MOM!" screamed Peter.

Henry walked.

And walked.

And walked.

His legs felt heavier, and heavier, and heavier.

"This field is muddy," moaned Henry.

"I'm bored," groaned Henry.

"My feet hurt," complained Henry.

"Can't we go home? We've already walked miles," whined Henry.

"We've been walking for ten minutes," said Dad.

"Please can we go on walks more often," said Perfect Peter. "Oh, look at those fluffy little sheepies!"

Horrid Henry pounced. He was a zombie biting the head off the hapless human.

"AAAAEEEEEE!" squealed Peter.

"Henry!" screamed Mom.

"Stop it!" screamed Dad. "Or no TV for a week."

When he was king, thought Horrid Henry, any parent who made their children go on a hike would be dumped barefoot in a scorpion-infested desert.

Plod.
Plod.
Plod.

Horrid Henry dragged his feet. Maybe his horrible mean parents would get fed up waiting for him and turn back, he thought, kicking some moldy leaves.

Squelch.

Squelch.

Squelch.

Oh no, not *another* muddy meadow.

And then suddenly Horrid Henry had
an idea. What was he thinking? All that
fresh air must be rotting his brain. The
sooner they got to the stupid lake, the
sooner they could get home for *Rapper
Zapper Zaps Terminator Gladiator*.

"Come on, everyone, let's run!"
shrieked Henry. "Race you down the
hill to the lake!"

"That's the spirit, Henry," said Dad.

Horrid Henry dashed
past Dad.

"OW!"
shrieked Dad,
tumbling into
the stinging
nettles.

159

Horrid Henry whizzed
past Mom.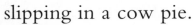
"Eww!"
shrieked
Mom,
slipping in a cow pie.
Splat!

Horrid Henry pushed past Peter.

"Waaa!" wailed Peter. "My boots are
getting dirty."

Horrid Henry scampered down the
muddy path.

"Wait Henry!" yelped Mom. "It's too slipp—aaaiiieeeee!"

Mom slid down the path on her bottom.

"Slow down!" puffed Dad.

"I can't run that fast," wailed Peter.

But Horrid Henry raced on.

"Shortcut across the field!" he called. "Come on slowpokes!" The black and white cow grazing alone in the middle raised its head.

"Henry!" shouted Dad.

Horrid Henry kept running.

"I don't think that's a cow!" shouted Mom.

The cow lowered its head and charged.

"It's a bull!" yelped Mom and Dad.
"RUN!"

"I said it was dangerous in the
countryside!" gasped Henry, as
everyone clambered over the fence in
the nick of time. "Look, there's the
lake!" he added, pointing.

Henry ran down to the water's edge.
Peter followed. The embankment
narrowed to a point. Peter slipped past
Henry and snagged the best spot, right
at the water's edge where the ducks
gathered.

"Hey, get away from there," said
Henry.

"I want to feed the ducks," said Peter.

"I want to feed the ducks," said
Henry. "Now move."

"I was here first," said Peter.

"Not any more," said Henry.

Horrid Henry pushed Peter.

"Out of my way, worm!"
Perfect Peter pushed him back.
"Don't call me worm!"
Henry wobbled.
Peter wobbled.
Splash!
Peter tumbled into the lake.
Crash!
Henry tumbled into
the lake.
"My babies!" shrieked
Mom, jumping in
after them.

"My—glug glug glug!" shrieked Dad,
jumping into the muddy water after her.
"My new boots!" gurgled Perfect Peter.

163

Bang!

Pow!

Terminator Gladiator slashed at Rapper Zapper.

Zap!

Rapper Zapper slashed back.

"Go Zappy!" yelled Henry, lying bundled up in blankets on the sofa. Once everyone had scrambled out of the lake, Mom and Dad wanted to get home as fast as possible.

"I think the park next time," mumbled Dad, sneezing.

"Definitely," mumbled Mom, coughing.

"Oh, I don't know," said Horrid Henry happily. "A little water never hurt anyone."

HORRID HENRY
WAKES THE DEAD

. . . .

"No, no, no, no, no!" shouted Miss
Battle-Axe. "Spitting is not a talent,
Graham. Violet, you can't do the
cancan as your talent. Ralph, burping
to the beat is not a talent."

She turned to Bert. "What's your
talent?"

"I dunno," said Beefy Bert.

"And what about you, Steven?" said
Miss Battle-Axe grimly.

"Caveman," grunted Stone-Age
Steven. "Ugg!"

Horrid Henry had had enough.

"Me next!" shrieked Horrid Henry. "I've got a great talent! Me next!"

"Me!" shrieked Moody Margaret.

"Me!" shrieked Rude Ralph.

"No one who shouts out will be performing *anything*," said Miss Battle-Axe.

Next week was Horrid Henry's school talent show. But this wasn't an ordinary school talent show. Oh no. This year was different. This year, the famous TV presenter Sneering Simone was choosing the winner.

But best and most fantastic of all,

the prize was a chance to appear on Simone's TV show, *Talent Tigers*. And from there…well, there was no end to the fame and fortune that awaited the winner.

Horrid Henry had to win. He just had to. A chance to be on TV! A chance for his genius to be recognized, at last.

The only problem was, he had so many talents it was impossible to pick just one. He could eat chips faster than Greedy Graham. He could burp to the theme tune of *Marvin the Maniac*. He could stick out his tongue almost as far as Moody Margaret.

But brilliant as these talents were, perhaps they weren't *quite* special enough to win. Hmmmm…

Wait, he had it.

He could perform his new rap, "I have

an ugly brother, ick ick ick/A smelly
toad brother, who makes me sick."
That would be sure to get him
on *Talent Tigers*.

"Margaret!" barked Miss Battle-Axe,
"what's your talent?"

"Susan and I are doing a rap," said
Moody Margaret.

What?

"*I'm* doing a rap," howled Henry.
How dare Margaret steal his idea!

"Only one person can do a rap," said
Miss Battle-Axe firmly.

"Unfair!" shrieked Horrid Henry.

"Be quiet, Henry," said Miss Battle-
Axe.

Moody Margaret stuck out her tongue
at Horrid Henry. "Nah nah ne nah nah."

Horrid Henry stuck out his tongue at
Moody Margaret. Aaaarrgh! It was so
unfair.

"I'm doing a hundred push-ups," said
Aerobic Al.

"I'm playing the drums," said Jazzy Jim.

"I want to do a rap!" howled Horrid
Henry. "Mine's much better than hers!"

"You have to do something else or
not take part," said Miss Battle-Axe,
consulting her list.

Not take part? Was Miss Battle-Axe out of her mind? Had all those years working on a chain gang done her in?

Miss Battle-Axe stood in front of Henry, baring her fangs. Her pen tapped impatiently on her notebook.

"Last chance, Henry. List closes in ten seconds..."

What to do, what to do?

"I'll do magic," said Horrid Henry.

How hard could it be to do some magic? He wasn't a master of disguise and the fearless leader of the Purple Hand Gang for nothing. In fact, not only would he do magic, he would do the greatest magic trick the world had ever seen. No rabbits out of a hat. No flowers out of a cane. No sawing a girl in half—though if Margaret volunteered Henry would be very happy to oblige.

No! He, Henry, Il Stupendioso, the greatest magician ever, would… would…he would wake the dead.

173

Wow. That was much cooler than a rap. He could see it now. He would chant his magic spells and wave his magic wand, until slowly, slowly, slowly, out of the coffin the bony body would rise, sending the audience screaming out of the hall!

Yes! thought Horrid Henry, *Talent Tigers* here I come. All he needed was an assistant.

Unfortunately, no one in his class wanted to assist him.

"Are you crazy?" said Gorgeous Gurinder.

"I've got a much better talent than
that. No way," said Clever Clare.

"Wake the dead?" gasped Weepy
William. "Nooooo."

Rats, thought Horrid Henry. For his
spectacular trick to work, an assistant
was essential. Henry hated working
with other children, but sometimes it
couldn't be helped. Was there anyone
he knew who would do exactly as they
were told? Someone who would obey
his every order? Hmmm. Perhaps there
was a certain someone who would
even pay for the privilege of being
in his show.

Perfect Peter was busy emptying the
dishwasher without being asked.

"Peter," said Henry sweetly, "how
much would you pay me if I let you be
in my magic show?"

Perfect Peter couldn't believe his ears.

Henry was asking him to be in his show. Peter had always wanted to be in a show. And now Henry was actually asking him after he'd said no a million times. It was a dream come true. He'd pay anything.

"I've got $6.27 in my piggy bank," said Peter eagerly.

Horrid Henry pretended to think.

"Done!" said Horrid Henry. "You can start by painting the coffin black."

"Thank you, Henry," said Peter humbly, handing over the money.

Tee-hee, thought Horrid Henry, pocketing the loot.

Henry told Peter what he had to do. Peter's jaw dropped.

"And will my name be on the billboard so everyone will know I'm your assistant?" asked Peter.

"Of course," said Horrid Henry.

★ ★ ★

The great day arrived at last. Henry had practiced and practiced and practiced. His magic robes were ready. His magic spells were ready. His coffin was ready. His props were ready. Even his dead body was as ready as it would ever be. Victory was his!

Henry and Peter stood backstage and peeked through the curtain as the audience charged into the hall. The school was buzzing. Parents pushed and shoved to get the best seats. There was a stir as Sneering Simone swept in, taking her seat in the front row.

"Would you *please* move?" demanded

Margaret's mother, waving her camcorder. "I can't see my little Maggie Muffin."

"And I can't see Al with *your* big head in the way," snapped Aerobic Al's dad, shoving his camera in front of Moody Margaret's mom.

"Parents, behave!" shouted Mrs. Oddbod. "What an exciting show we have for you today! You will be amazed at all the talents in this school. First Clare will recite Pi, which as you all know is the ratio of the circumference of a circle to the diameter, to 31 significant figures!"

"3.14159 26535 89793 23846 26433 83279," said Clever Clare.

Sneering Simone made a few notes.

"Boring," shouted Horrid Henry. "Boring!"

"Shhh," hissed Miss Battle-Axe.

"Now, Gurinder, Linda, Fiona, and Zoe proudly present: the cushion dance!"

Gorgeous Gurinder, Lazy Linda, Fiery Fiona, and Zippy Zoe ran on stage and placed a cushion in each corner. Then they skipped to each pillow, pretended to sew it, then hopped around with a pillow each, singing:

"We're the stitching queens
    dressed in sateen,
    we're full of beans,
    see us preen,
    as we steal...the...scene!"

Sneering Simone looked surprised. Tee-hee, thought Horrid Henry gleefully. If everyone's talents were as awful as that, he was a shoe-in for *Talent Tigers*.

"Lovely," said Mrs. Oddbod. "Just lovely. And now we have William, who will play the flute."

Weepy William put his mouth to the flute and blew. There was no sound.

William stopped and stared at his flute. The mouth hole appeared to have vanished.

Everyone was looking at him. What could he do?

"Toot toot toot," trilled William, pretending to blow. "Toot toot toot— waaaaaah!" wailed William, bursting into tears and running off stage.

"Never mind," said Mrs. Oddbod, "anyone could put the mouthpiece on upside down. And now we have…" Mrs. Oddbod glanced at her paper, "a caveman Ugga Ugg dance."

Stone-Age Steven and Beefy Bert stomped on stage wearing leopard-skin costumes and carrying clubs.

"UGGG!" grunted Stone-Age Steven. "UGGG UGGG UGGG UGGG UGGG! Me caveman!"

STOMP CLUMPA CLUMP
STOMP CLUMPA CLUMP
stomped Stone-Age Steven.

STOMP CLUMPA CLUMP
STOMP CLUMPA CLUMP
stomped Beefy Bert.

"UGGA BUG UGGA BUG UGG UGG UGG," bellowed Steven, whacking the floor with his club.

"Bert!" hissed Miss Battle-Axe. "This isn't your talent! What are you doing on stage?"

"I dunno," said Beefy Bert.

"Boo! Boooooo!" jeered Horrid Henry from backstage as the cavemen thudded off.

Then Moody Margaret and Sour Susan performed their rap:

182

"Mar-garet, ooh ooh oooh
Mar-garet, it's all true
Mar-garet, best of the best
Pick Margaret, and dump the rest."

Rats, thought Horrid Henry, glaring. My rap was so much better. What a waste. And why was the audience applauding?

"Booooo!" yelled Horrid Henry. "Boooooo!"

"Another sound out of you and you will not be performing," snapped Miss Battle-Axe.

"And now Soraya will be singing 'You Broke My Heart in 39 Pieces,' accompanied by her mother on the piano," said Mrs. Oddbod hastily.

"Sing out, Soraya!" hissed her mother, pounding the piano and singing along.

"I'm singing as loud as I can," yelled Soraya.

BANG! BANG! BANG! BANG!
BANG! BANG! went the piano.

Then Jolly Josh began to saw "Twinkle,
Twinkle Little Star" on his double bass.
Sneering Simone held her ears.

"We're next," said Horrid Henry,
grabbing hold of his billboard and
whipping off the cloth.

Perfect Peter stared at the billboard.
It read:

Il Stupendioso, world's greatest
magician played by Henry

Magic by Henry
Costumes by Henry
Props by Henry
Sound by Henry
written by Henry
Directed by Henry

"But Henry," said Peter, "where's my name?"

"Right here," said Horrid Henry, pointing.

On the back, in tiny letters, was written:

Assistant: Peter

"But no one will see that," said Peter. Henry snorted.

"If I put your name on the *front* of the billboard, everyone would guess the trick," said Henry.

"No they wouldn't," said Peter.

Honestly, thought Horrid Henry, did any magician ever have such a dreadful helper?

"I'm the star," said Henry. "You're lucky you're even in my show. Now shut up and get in the coffin."

Perfect Peter was furious. That was just like Henry, to be so mean.

"Get in!" ordered Henry.

Peter put on his skeleton mask and climbed into the coffin. He was fuming.

Henry had said he'd put his name on the billboard, and then he'd written it on the back. No one would know he was the assistant. No one.

The lights dimmed. Spooky music began to play.

"Ooooooooohhhh," moaned the ghostly sounds as Horrid Henry, wearing his special long black robes studded with stars and a special magician's hat, dragged his coffin through the curtains onto the stage.

"I am Il Stupendioso, the great and powerful magician!" intoned Henry. "Now, Il Stupendioso will perform the greatest trick ever seen. Be prepared to marvel. Be prepared to be amazed. Be prepared not to believe your eyes. I, Il Stupendioso, will wake the dead!!"

"Ooohh," gasped the audience.

Horrid Henry swept back and forth across the stage, waving his wand and mumbling.

"First I will say the secret words of magic. Beware! Beware! Do not try this at home. Do not try this in a graveyard. Do not—" Henry's voice sank to a whisper—"do not try this unless you're prepared for the dead...to walk!" Horrid Henry ended his sentence with a blood-curdling scream. The audience gasped.

Horrid Henry stood above the coffin and chanted:

"Abracadabra,
flummery flax,

voodoo hoodoo
mumbo crax.
Rise and shine, corpse of mine!"

Then Horrid Henry whacked the
coffin once with his wand.

Slowly, Perfect Peter poked a
skeleton hand out of the coffin, then
withdrew it.

"Ohhhh," went
the audience.
Toddler Tom
began to wail.

Horrid Henry
repeated the spell.

"Abracadabra,
flummery flax,
voodoo hoodoo
mumbo crax.
Rise and shine, bony swine!"

Then Horrid Henry whacked the coffin twice with his wand.

This time Perfect Peter slowly raised the plastic skull with a few tufts of blond hair glued to it, then lowered it back down. Toddler Tom began to howl.

"And now, for the third and final time, I will say the magic spell, and before your eyes, the body will rise. Stand back…"

"Abracadabra,
flummery flax,
voodoo hoodoo
mumbo crax.
Rise and shine, here is the sign!"

And Horrid Henry whacked the coffin three times with his wand.

The audience held its breath.
And held it.
And held it.
And held it.
"He's been dead a long time, maybe his hearing isn't so good," said Horrid Henry. "Rise and shine, here is the sign," shouted Henry, whacking the coffin furiously.

Again, nothing happened.

"Rise and shine, brother of mine," hissed Henry, kicking the coffin, "or you'll be sorry you were born."

I'm on strike, thought Perfect Peter. How dare Henry stick his name on the back of the billboard. And after all Peter's hard work!

Horrid Henry looked at the audience. The audience looked expectantly at Horrid Henry.

What could he do? Open the coffin and yank the body out? Yell, "Ta-da!" and run off stage? Do his famous elephant dance?

Horrid Henry took a deep breath.

"Now that's what I call *dead*," said Horrid Henry.

"This was a difficult decision," said Sneering Simone. Henry held his breath. He'd kill Peter later. Peter had finally

risen from the coffin *after* Henry left
the stage, then instead of slinking off,
he'd actually said, "Hello everyone! I'm
alive!" and waved. Grrr. Well, Peter
wouldn't have to pretend to be a corpse
once Henry had finished with him.

"...a very difficult decision. But I've
decided that the winner is..." Please not
Margaret, please not Margaret, prayed
Henry. Sneering Simone consulted
her notes, "The winner is the Il
Stupendioso—"

"YES!!" screamed Horrid Henry,
leaping to his feet. He'd done it! Fame
at last! Henry Superstar was born! Yes,
yes, yes!

Sneering Simone glared. "As I was
saying, the Il Stupendioso corpse.
Great comic timing. Can someone tell
me his name?"

Horrid Henry stopped dancing.

Huh?

What?

The *corpse?*

"Is that me?" said Peter. "*I* won?"

"NOOOOOOOOO!" shrieked Horrid Henry.

MOODY MARGARET'S SLEEPOVER

· ·

"What are you doing here?" said
Moody Margaret, glaring.

"I'm here for the sleepover," said
Sour Susan, glaring back.

"You were uninvited, remember?"
said Margaret.

"And then you invited me again,
remember?" snapped Susan.

"Did not."

"Did too. You told me last week I
could come."

"Did not."

"Did too. You're such a meanie,

Margaret," scowled Susan. Aaaarrggghh.
Why was she friends with such a moody
old grouch?

Moody Margaret heaved a heavy sigh.
Why was she friends with such a sour
old slop bucket?

"Well, since you're here, I guess
you'd better come in," said Margaret.
"But don't expect any dessert 'cause
there won't be enough for you and
my *real* guests."

Sour Susan stomped inside Margaret's
house. Grrrr. She wouldn't be inviting
Margaret to her next sleepover party,
that's for sure.

Horrid Henry couldn't sleep. He was
hot. He was hungry.

"Cookies!" moaned his tummy. "Give
me cookies!"

Because Mom and Dad were the

meanest, most horrible
parents in the
world, they'd
forgotten to buy
more cookies
and there wasn't
a single solitary
crumb in the house.
Henry knew because he'd
searched everywhere.

"Give me cookies!" growled his
tummy. "What are you waiting for?"

I'm going to die of hunger up here,
thought Horrid Henry. And it will be
all Mom and Dad's fault. They'll come
in tomorrow morning and find just a
few wisps of hair and some teeth. Then
they'd be sorry. Then they'd wail and
gnash. But it would be too late.

"How could we have forgotten to buy
chocolate cookies?" Dad would sob.

"We deserve to be locked up forever!" Mom would shriek.

"And now there's nothing left of Henry but a tooth, and it's all our fault!" they'd howl.

Humph. Serve them right.

Wait. What an idiot he was. Why should he risk death from starvation when he knew where there was a rich stash of all sorts of yummy cookies waiting just for him?

Moody Margaret's Secret Club tent was sure to be full to bursting with

200

goodies! Horrid Henry hadn't raided it in ages. And so long as he was quick, no one would ever know he'd left the house.

"Go on, Henry," urged his tummy. "FEED ME!"

Horrid Henry didn't need to be urged twice.

Slowly, quietly, he sneaked out of bed, crept down the stairs, and tiptoed out of the back door. Then quick over the wall, and ta-da, he was in the Secret Club tent. There was Margaret's Secret Club cookie tin, in her pathetic hiding place under a blanket. Ha!

Horrid Henry prized open the lid. Oh wow. It was filled to the brim with

Chocolate Fudge Chewies! And those scrumptious Triple Chocolate Chip Marshmallow Squidgies! Henry scooped up a huge handful and stuffed them in his mouth.

Chomp. Chomp. Chomp.

Oh wow. Oh wow. Was there anything more delicious in the whole wide world than a mouthful of stolen cookies?

"More! More! More!" yelped his tummy.

Who was Horrid Henry to say no?

Henry reached in to snatch another mega handful...

BANG! SLAM! BANG!

STOMP! STOMP! STOMP!

"That's too bad, Gurinder," snapped Margaret's voice. "It's my party so I decide. Hurry up, Susan."

"I am hurrying," said Susan's voice.

The footsteps were heading straight for the Secret Club tent.

Yikes. What was Margaret doing outside at this time of night? There wasn't a moment to lose.

Horrid Henry looked around wildly. Where could he hide? There was a wicker chest at the back, where Margaret kept her dress-up clothes. Horrid Henry leaped inside and pulled the lid shut. Hopefully, the girls wouldn't be long and he could escape

home before Mom and Dad discovered
he'd been out.

Moody Margaret bustled into the
tent, followed by her mother, Gorgeous
Gurinder, Kung-Fu Kate, Lazy Linda,
Vain Violet, Singing Soraya, and
Sour Susan.
   "Now, girls, it's late, I want you to go
straight to bed, lights out, no talking,"
said Margaret's mother. "My little Maggie
Moo Moo needs her beauty sleep."

Ha, thought Horrid Henry. Margaret could sleep for a thousand years and she'd still look like a frog.

"Yes, Mom," said Margaret.

"Good night, girls," trilled Margaret's mom. "See you in the morning."

Phew, thought Horrid Henry, lying as still as he could. He'd be back home in no time, mission safely accomplished.

"We're sleeping out here?" said Singing Soraya. "In a tent?"

"I said it was a Secret Club sleepover," said Margaret.

Horrid Henry's heart sank. Huh? They were planning to sleep here? Rats, rats, rats, double rats. He was going to have to hide inside this hot dusty chest until they were asleep.

Maybe they'd all fall asleep soon, thought Horrid Henry hopefully.

Because he had to get home before Mom and Dad discovered he was missing. If they realized he'd sneaked outside, he'd be in so much trouble his life wouldn't be worth living and he might as well abandon all hope of ever watching TV or eating another cookie until he was an old, shriveled bag of bones struggling to chew with his one tooth and watch TV with his magnifying glass and hearing aid. Yikes!

Horrid Henry looked grimly at the cookies clutched in his fist. Thank goodness he'd brought provisions.

He might be trapped here for a very
long time.

"Where's your sleeping bag, Violet?"
said Margaret.

"I didn't bring one," said Vain Violet.
"I don't like sleeping on the floor."

"Tough," said Margaret, "that's where
we're sleeping."

"But I need to sleep in a bed,"
whined Vain Violet. "I don't want to
sleep out here."

"Well, we do," said Margaret.

"Yeah," said Susan.

"I can sleep anywhere," said Lazy
Linda, yawning.

"I'm calling my mom," said Violet.
"I want to go home."

"Go ahead," said Margaret. "We
don't need you, do we?"

Silence.

"Oh come on, Violet, stay," said
Gurinder.

"Yeah, stay," said Kung-Fu Kate.

"No!" said Violet, flouncing out of
the tent.

"Hummph," said Moody Margaret.

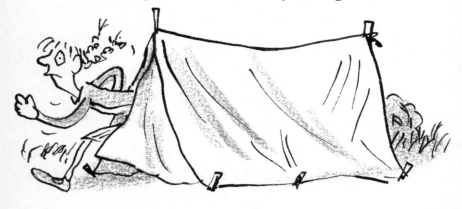

"She's no fun anyway. Now, everyone put your sleeping bags down where I say. I need to sleep by the entrance, because I need fresh air."

"I want to sleep by the entrance," said Soraya.

"No," said Margaret, "it's my party so I decide. Susan, you go to the back because you snore."

"Do not," said Susan.

"Do too," said Margaret.

"Liar."

"Liar."

SLAP!

SLAP!

"That's it!" wailed Susan. "I'm calling my mom."

"Go ahead," said Margaret, "see if I care, snore-box. That'll be tons more Chocolate Fudge Chewies for the rest of us."

Sour Susan stood still. She'd been looking forward to Margaret's sleepover for ages. And she still hadn't had any of the midnight feast Margaret had promised.

"All right, I'll stay," said Susan sourly, putting her sleeping bag down at the back of the tent by the dress-up chest.

"I want to be next to Gurinder," said Lazy Linda, scratching her head.

"Do you have lice?" said Gurinder.

"No!" said Linda.

"You do too," said Gurinder.

"Do not," said Linda.

"Do too," said Gurinder. "I'm not sleeping next to someone who has lice."

"Me neither," said Kate.

"Me neither," said Soraya.

"Don't look at me," said Margaret. "I'm not sleeping next to you."

"I don't have lice!" wailed Linda.

"Go next to Susan," said Margaret.

"But she snores," protested Linda.

"But she has lice," protested Susan.

"Do not."

"Do not."

"Bedbug head."

"Snory!"

Suddenly something scuttled across the floor.

"EEEEK!" squealed Soraya. "It's a mouse!" She scrambled onto the dress-up chest. The lid sagged.

"It won't hurt you," said Margaret.

"Yeah," said Susan.

"Eeeek!" squealed Linda, shrinking back. The lid sagged even more.

Cree—eaaak went the chest.

Aaarrrrggghhh, thought Horrid Henry, trying to squash himself down before he was squished.

"Eeeek!" squealed Gurinder, scrambling onto the chest.

CREE—EAAAAAK! went the chest.

Errrrgh, thought Horrid Henry, pushing up against the sagging lid as hard as he could.

"I can't sleep if there's a...mouse," said Gurinder. She looked around nervously. "What if it runs on top of my sleeping bag?"

Margaret sighed. "It's only a mouse," she said.

"I'm scared of mice," whimpered Gurinder. "I'm leaving!" And she ran out of the tent, wailing.

"More food for the rest of us," said Margaret, shrugging. "I say we feast now."

"About time," said Soraya.

"Let's start with the Chocolate Fudge Chewies," said Margaret, opening the Secret Club cookie tin. "Everyone can

have two, except for me, I get four
'cause it's my…"

Margaret peered into the tin. There
were only a few crumbs inside.

"Who stole the cookies?" said
Margaret.

"Wasn't me," said Susan.

"Wasn't me," said Soraya.

"Wasn't me," said Kate.

"Wasn't me," said Linda.

Tee-hee, thought Horrid Henry.

"One of you did, so no one is getting anything to eat until you admit it," snapped Margaret.

"Meanie," muttered Susan sourly.

"What did you say?" said Moody Margaret.

"Nothing," said Susan.

"Then we'll just have to wait for the culprit to come forward," said Margaret, scowling. "Meanwhile, get in your sleeping bags. We're going to tell scary stories in the dark. Who knows a good one?"

"I do," said Susan.

"Not the story about the ghost kitty cat that drank up all the milk in your kitchen, is it?" said Margaret.

Susan scowled.

"Well, it's a true scary story," said Susan.

"I know a real scary story," said Kung-Fu Kate. "It's about this monster—"

"Mine's better," said Margaret. "It's about a flesh-eating zombie that creeps around at night and rips off—"

"NOOOO," wailed Linda. "I hate being scared. I'm calling my mom to come and get me."

"No scaredy-cats allowed in the Secret Club," said Margaret.

"I don't care," said Linda, flouncing out.

"It's not a sleepover unless we tell ghost stories," said Moody Margaret. "Turn off your flashlights. It won't be scary unless we're all sitting in the dark."

Sniffle. Sniffle. Sniffle.

"I want to go home," sniveled Soraya.

"I've never slept away from home
before...I want my mommy."

"What a baby," said Moody Margaret.

Horrid Henry was cramped and hot and
uncomfortable. Pins and needles were
shooting up his arm. He shifted his
shoulder, brushing against the lid.

There was a muffled creak.

Henry froze. Whoops. Henry prayed
they hadn't heard anything.

"...and the zombie crept inside the
tent, gnashing its bloody teeth and
sniffing the air for human flesh, hungry
for more—"

Ow. His poor aching arm. Henry
shifted position again.

Creak...

"What was that?" whispered Susan.

"What was what?" said Margaret.

"There was a...a...creak..." said Susan.

"The wind," said Margaret. "Anyway,
the zombie sneaked into the tent and—"
"You don't think…" hissed Kate.
"Think what?" said Margaret.
"That the zombie…the zombie…"

I'm starving, thought Horrid Henry.

I'll just eat a few cookies really, really, really quietly—

Crunch. Crunch.

"What was that?" whispered Susan.

"What was what?" said Margaret. "You're ruining the story."

"That...crunching sound," hissed Susan.

Horrid Henry gasped. What an idiot he was! Why hadn't he thought of this before?

Crunch. Crunch. Crunch.

"Like someone...someone...crunching on...bones," whispered Kung-Fu Kate.

"Someone...here..." whispered Susan.

Tap. Horrid Henry rapped on the underside of the lid.

Tap! Tap! Tap!

"I didn't hear anything," said Margaret loudly.

"It's the zombie!" screamed Susan.

"He's in here!" screamed Kate.
AAAAARRRRRRRGHHHHHHH!"

"I'm going home!"
screamed Susan and Kate.
"MOMMMMMMMMMYYYY!" they
wailed, running off.

Ha ha, thought Horrid Henry. His
brilliant plan had worked!!! Tee-hee.
He'd hop out, steal the rest of the feast
and scoot home. Hopefully Mom
and Dad—
YANK!

Suddenly the chest lid was flung
open and a flashlight shone in his eyes.

Moody Margaret's hideous face glared
down at him.

"Gotcha!" said Moody Margaret.
"Oh boy, are you in trouble. Just
wait till I tell on you. Ha ha, Henry,
you're dead."

Horrid Henry climbed out of the
chest and brushed a few crumbs onto
the rug.

"Just wait till I tell everyone at school
about your sleepover," said Horrid
Henry. "How you were so mean and
bossy everyone ran away."

"Your parents will punish you
forever," said Moody Margaret.

"Your name will be mud forever,"
said Horrid Henry. "Everyone will
laugh at you and serves you right,
Maggie Moo Moo."

"Don't call me that," said Margaret,
glaring.

"Call you what, Moo Moo?"

"All right," said Margaret slowly. "I won't tell on you if you give me two packs of Chocolate Fudge Chewies."

"No way," said Henry. "I won't tell on you if you give me three packs of Chocolate Fudge Chewies."

"Fine," said Margaret. "Your parents are still up, I'll tell them where you are right now. I wouldn't want them to worry."

"Go ahead," said Henry. "I can't wait until school tomorrow."

Margaret scowled.

"Just this once," said Horrid Henry. "I won't tell on you if you won't tell on me."

"Just this once," said Moody Margaret. "But never again."

They glared at each other.

When he was king, thought Horrid

Henry, anyone named Margaret would be catapulted over the walls into an oozy swamp. Meanwhile...on guard, Margaret. On guard. I will be avenged!

HORRID HENRY
AND THE
ABOMINABLE SNOWMAN

Moody Margaret took aim.

Thwack!

A snowball whizzed past and smacked Sour Susan in the face.

"AAAAARRGGHHH!" shrieked Susan.

"Ha ha, got you," said Margaret.

"You big meanie," howled Susan, scooping up a fistful of snow and hurling it at Margaret.

Thwack!

Susan's snowball smacked Moody Margaret in the face.

"OWWWW!" screamed Margaret. "You've blinded me."

"Good!" screamed Susan.

"I hate you!" shouted Margaret, shoving Susan.

"I hate you more!" shouted Susan, pushing Margaret.

Splat! Margaret toppled into the snow.

Splat! Susan toppled into the snow.

"I'm going home to build my own snowman," sobbed Susan.

"Fine. I'll win without you," said Margaret.

"Will not!"

"Will too! I'm going to win, copycat," shrieked Margaret.

"*I'm* going to win," shrieked Susan. "I kept my best ideas secret."

"Win? Win what?" demanded Horrid Henry, stomping down his front steps in his snow boots and swaggering over.

Henry could hear the word *win* from miles away.

"Haven't you heard about the competition?" said Sour Susan. "The prize is—"

"Shut up! Don't tell him," shouted Moody Margaret, packing snow onto her snowman's head.

Win? Competition? Prize? Horrid

Henry's ears quivered. What secret were they trying to keep from him? Well, not for long. Horrid Henry was an expert at extracting information.

"Oh, the competition. I know all about *that*," lied Horrid Henry. "Hey, great snowman," he added, strolling casually over to Margaret's snowman and pretending to admire her work.

Now, what should he do? Torture? Margaret's ponytail was always a tempting target. And snow down her sweater would make her talk.

What about blackmail? He could spread some great rumors about Margaret at school. Or…

"Tell me about the competition or the ice guy gets it," said Horrid Henry suddenly, leaping over to the snowman and putting his hands around its neck.

"You wouldn't dare," gasped Moody
Margaret.

Henry's mittened hands got ready
to push.

"Bye bye, head," hissed Horrid
Henry. "Nice knowing you."

Margaret's snowman wobbled.

"Stop!" screamed Margaret. "I'll tell
you. It doesn't matter 'cause you'll never
ever win."

"Keep talking," said Horrid Henry

warily, watching out in case Susan tried to ambush him from behind.

"Frosty Freeze is having a best snowman competition," said Moody Margaret, glaring. "The winner gets a year's free supply of ice cream. The judges will decide tomorrow morning. Now get away from my snowman."

Horrid Henry walked off in a daze, his jaw dropping. Margaret and Susan pelted him with snowballs but Henry didn't even notice. Free ice cream for a year direct from the Frosty Freeze Ice Cream factory. Oh wow! Horrid Henry couldn't believe it. Mom and Dad were so mean and horrible they hardly ever let him have ice cream. And when they did, they never *ever* let him put on his own hot fudge sauce and whipped cream and sprinkles. Or even scoop the ice cream himself. Oh no.

Well, when he won the Best Snowman Competition they couldn't stop him from gorging on Chunky Chocolate Fab Fudge Caramel Delight or Vanilla Whip Tutti-Frutti Toffee Treat. Oh boy! Henry could taste that glorious ice cream now. He'd live on ice cream. He'd bathe in ice cream. He'd sleep in ice cream. Everyone from school would turn up at his house when the Frosty Freeze truck arrived bringing his weekly barrels. No matter how much they begged, Horrid Henry

would send them all away. No way was
he sharing a drop of his precious ice
cream with *anyone.*

And all he had to do was build the best
snowman in the neighborhood. Pah!
Henry's was sure to be the winner. He
would build the biggest snowman of all.
And not just a snowman. A snowman
with claws and horns and fangs. A
vampire-demon-monster snowman. An
Abominable Snowman. Yes!

Henry watched Margaret and Susan
rolling snow and packing their saggy
snowman. Ha. Snow heap, more like.

"You'll never win with *that*," jeered
Horrid Henry. "Your snowman is
pathetic."

"Better than yours," snapped Margaret.

Horrid Henry rolled his eyes.

"Obviously, because I haven't started
mine yet."

"We've got a big head start on you, so ha ha ha," said Susan. "We're building a ballerina snowgirl."

"Shut up, Susan," screamed Margaret.

A ballerina snowgirl? What a stupid idea. If that was the best they could do, Henry was sure to win.

"Mine will be the biggest, the best, the most gigantic snowman ever seen," said Horrid Henry. "And much better than your stupid snow dwarf."

"Fat chance," sneered Margaret.

"Yeah, Henry," sneered Susan. "Ours is the best."

"No way," said Horrid Henry, starting to roll a gigantic ball of snow for Abominable's big belly. There was no time to lose.

Up the path, down the path, across the garden, down the side, back and forth, back and forth, Horrid Henry rolled the biggest ball of snow ever seen.

"Henry, can I build a snowman with you?" came a little voice.

"No," said Henry, starting to carve out some clawed feet.

"Oh please," said Peter. "We could build a great big one together. Like a bunny snowman, or a—"

"No!" said Henry. "It's *my* snowman. Build your own."

"Moooommmm!" wailed Peter. "Henry won't let me build a snowman with him."

"Don't be horrid, Henry," said Mom. "Why don't you build one together?"

"NO!!!" said Horrid Henry. He wanted to make his *own* snowman.

If he built a snowman with his stupid worm brother, he'd have to share the prize. Well, no way. He wanted all that ice cream for himself. And his Abominable Snowman was sure to be the best. Why share a prize when you didn't have to?

"Get away from my snowman, Peter," hissed Henry.

Perfect Peter sniveled. Then he started
to roll a tiny ball of snow.

"And get your own snow," said
Henry. "All this is mine."

"Mooooom!" wailed Peter. "Henry's
hogging all the snow."

"We're done," trilled Moody Margaret.
"Beat *this* if you can."

Horrid Henry looked at Margaret and
Susan's snowgirl, complete with a big
pink tutu wound around the waist. It was
as big as Margaret.

"That old heap of snow is nothing
compared to *mine*," bragged Horrid Henry.

Moody Margaret and Sour Susan looked
at Henry's Abominable Snowman,

238

complete with horned Viking helmet,
fangs, and hairy scary claws. It was a few
inches taller than Henry.

"Nah nah ne nah nah, mine's bigger,"
boasted Henry.

"Nah nah ne nah nah, mine's better,"
boasted Margaret.

"How do you like *my* snowman?"
said Peter. "Do you think *I* could win?"

Horrid Henry stared at Perfect Peter's
tiny snowman. It didn't even have a
head, just a long, thin, lumpy body with
two stones stuck in the top for eyes.

Horrid Henry howled with laughter.

"That's the worst snowman I've ever seen," said Henry. "It doesn't even have a head. That's a snow carrot."

"It is not," wailed Peter. "It's a big bunny."

"Henry! Peter! Dinner time," called Mom.

Henry stuck out his tongue at Margaret.

"And don't you dare touch my snowman."

Margaret stuck out her tongue at Henry.

"And don't you dare touch *my* snowgirl."

"I'll be watching you, Margaret."

"I'll be watching *you*, Henry."

They glared at each other.

★ ★ ★

Henry woke.

What was that noise? Was Margaret sabotaging his snowman? Was Susan stealing his snow?

Horrid Henry dashed to the window.

Phew. There was his Abominable Snowman, big as ever, dwarfing every other snowman on the street. Henry's was definitely the biggest, and the best. Mmm boy, he could taste that Triple Fudge Gooey Chocolate Chip Peanut Butter Marshmallow Custard ice cream right now.

Horrid Henry climbed back into bed.

A tiny doubt nagged him.

Was his snowman *definitely* bigger than Margaret's?

'Course it was, thought Henry.

"Are you sure?" rumbled his tummy.

"Yeah," said Henry.

"Because I really want that ice cream," growled his tummy. "Why don't you double-check?"

Horrid Henry got out of bed.

He was sure his was bigger and better than Margaret's. He was absolutely sure his was bigger and better.

But what if—

I can't sleep without checking, thought Henry.

Tip toe.

Tip toe.

Tip toe.

Horrid Henry slipped out of the front door.

The whole street was silent and white and frosty. Every house had a snowman in front. All of them much smaller than Henry's, he noted with satisfaction.

And there was his Abominable Snowman looming up, Viking horns scraping the sky. Horrid Henry gazed at him proudly. Next to him was Peter's pathetic pimple, with its stupid black stones. A snow lump, thought Henry.

Then he looked over at Margaret's snowgirl. Maybe it had fallen down, thought Henry hopefully. And if it hadn't, maybe he could help it on its way…

He looked again. And again. That evil
fiend!

Margaret had sneaked an extra ball
of snow on top, complete with a huge
flowery hat.

That little cheater, thought Horrid
Henry indignantly. She'd sneaked out
after bedtime and made hers bigger than

244

his. How dare she? Well, he'd fix
Margaret. He'd add more snow to his
right away.

Horrid Henry looked around. Where
could he find more snow? He'd already
used up every drop on his front lawn
to build his giant, and no new snow
had fallen.

Henry shivered.

Brr, it was freezing. He needed more
snow, and he needed it fast. His slippers
were starting to feel very wet and cold.

Horrid Henry eyed Peter's pathetic

lump of snow. Hmmm, thought Horrid Henry.

Hmmm, thought Horrid Henry again.

Well, it's not doing any good sitting there, thought Henry. Someone could trip over it. Someone could hurt himself. In fact, Peter's snow lump was

a danger. He had to act fast before
someone fell over it and broke a leg.

Quickly, he scooped up Peter's
snowman and stacked it carefully on top
of his. Then, standing on his tippy-toes,
he balanced the Abominable Snowman's
Viking horns on top.

Ta-da!

Much better. And *much* bigger than
Margaret's.

Teeth chattering, Horrid Henry
sneaked back into his house and crept
into bed. Ice cream, here I come,
thought Horrid Henry.

Ding dong.

Horrid Henry jumped out of bed.
What a morning to oversleep.

Perfect Peter ran and opened the door.

"We're from the Frosty Freeze Ice
Cream Factory," said the man, beaming.

"And you've got the winning snowman out front."

"I won!" screeched Horrid Henry. "I won!" He tore down the stairs and out the door. Oh what a wonderful, wonderful day. The sky was blue. The sun was shining—huh???

Horrid Henry looked around.

Horrid Henry's Abominable Snowman was gone.

"Margaret!" screamed Henry. "I'll kill you!"

But Moody Margaret's snowgirl was gone too.

The Abominable Snowman's helmet lay on its side on the ground. All that was left of Henry's snowman was... Peter's pimple, with its two black stone eyes. A big blue ribbon was pinned to the top.

"But that's *my* snowman," said Perfect Peter.

"But...but..." said Horrid Henry.

"You mean, *I* won?" said Peter.

"That's wonderful, Peter," said Mom.

"That's fantastic, Peter," said Dad.

"All the others melted," said the Frosty Freeze man. "Yours was the only one left. It must have been a giant."

"It was," howled Horrid Henry.

And now it's time for some fun! Let's get started!

Horrid Henry Crossword Puzzle!

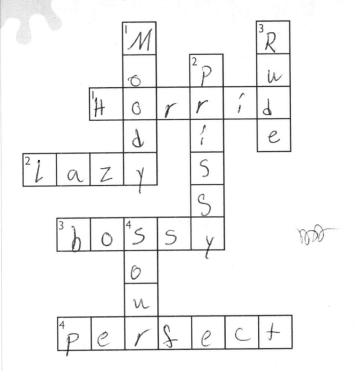

Across:
1. Horrid Henry
2. _____ Linda
3. _____ Bill
4. _____ Peter

Down:
1. _____ Margaret
2. _____ Polly
3. Rude Ralph
4. Sour Susan

Word Bank:

Bossy	Lazy	Perfect	Rude
Horrid	Moody	Prissy	Sour

Horrid Henry's Jokes

Where do ghosts go on vacation?

Death Valley.

What do vampires cross the sea in?

Blood vessels.

Henry: Knock knock.

Margaret: Who's there?

Henry: Boo.

Margaret: Boo who?

Henry: Don't cry, it's only a joke.

Write your favorite joke here:

_____

_____

_____

Draw a picture to go along with your joke.

Mess up Perfect Peter:
add your own

which one doesn't belong?

Even More Jokes!

Why did the Tyrannosaurus Rex go to the doctor?

He had a dino-sore

Why did the golfer wear two pairs of underpants?

In case he got a hole in one.

Miss Battle-Axe: Henry! If you multiplied 1497 by 371 what answer would you get?

Henry: The wrong one.

Draw your own
abominable Snowman

Coloring Fun!

Coloring Fun!

Write Your Own Song

Write a song about Henry using a popular tune like "I'm a Little Teapot" or "Take Me Out to the Ballgame"

Or, sing this song to the tune "Frère Jacques."

Horrid Henry
Horrid Henry
is bad news
is bad news
everywhere that he goes
trouble surely follows
Crash!
Smash!
Boom.
Crash!
Smash!
Boom.

You can make your own GLOP!

It's very simple to make your own disgusting, gooey, gross Glop. You can make Glop with anything you can find in the kitchen—the yuckier the better! Horrid Henry and Moody Margaret mixed oatmeal, vinegar, baked beans, moldy cheese, and even peanut butter into their icky Glop. If you want to make some simple Glop, try this basic recipe.

Ingredients

16 oz box of cornstarch

1 ½ cups water

Food coloring (optional)

Directions

Dump the cornstarch and water into a large bowl. Add about 15 or 20 drops of food coloring. Squish the Glop together with your hands until it's all mixed. Now gross out your little brother or sister by letting the Glop ooze through your fingers! Yuck!

About the Author

Photo: Francesco Guidicini

Francesca Simon spent her childhood on the beach in California and then went to Yale and Oxford Universities to study medieval history and literature. She now lives in London with her family. She has written over forty-five books and won the Children's Book of the Year in 2008 at the Galaxy British Book Awards for *Horrid Henry and the Abominable Snowman*.